MISTRESS

Iain Bard

MISTRESS

A DOUBLE DRAGON PAPERBACK

© Copyright 2020
Iain Bard

The right of Iain Bard to be identified as author of this work has been asserted in accordance with the Copyright, Designs and Patents Act 1988

All Rights Reserved

No reproduction, copy or transmission of the publication may be made without written permission. No paragraph of this publication may be reproduced, copied or transmitted save with the written permission of the publisher, or in accordance with the provisions of the Copyright Act 1956 (as amended).

Any person who does any unauthorised act in relation to this publication may be liable to criminal prosecution and civil claims for damages.

ISBN 978-1-78695-340-7

Double Dragon
is an imprint of
Fiction4All

Published 2020
Fiction4All
www.fiction4all.com

*

All night the witch sang
And the castle grew up from the rock
With tower and turrets crowned.
All night she sang,
And when fell the morning dew,
'Twas finished round and round.
Isle of Skye Legend

Origin and source unknown
*

    Dedicated to Gwen - my soul twin

Chapter One
Labor

Isle of Skye, Scotland
A.D. 1143

The night air was like a frigid hand that stroked his cheek with the cold and bitter touch of a jilted lover.

The biting sting on his face was not an unwelcome sensation. Mahrea's exceedingly long and arduous labor left him feeling powerless, disoriented, and numb as he kept a frustrating twelve-hour vigil outside her bedroom door. The midwife dismissed him some time ago, and although he was accustomed to giving orders rather than submitting to them, he gladly acquiesced to her suggestion to take a brief respite from his husbandly post.

He stood on the balcony of the highest castle tower. The frost-suffused breeze, shocking yet invigorating, rapidly aroused him from a weary and troubled fatigue. Paradoxically, the jolt of winter's icy breath on his face produced unexpected warmth which radiated through his core like a blazing and vigorous hearth-fire heating a dry and brittle ice-encased log ignited by the kindling spark of February's metaphorical match. In fact, he felt oddly revitalized. The warm excitement rushed through his yet youthful veins. A boiling cascade surged from the steaming reservoir of a hot spring instantly to thaw and supplant the frigid ennui gripping his heart since his ill-omened engagement to the frosty and remote Viking princess.

After Mahrea's collapse at mid-day, Rhys was extremely concerned for the well-being of his child in her belly. Although his servants did their best to make him comfortable as he waited in the small antechamber outside her bedroom, he understandably felt plagued with apprehension and foreboding.

"Ne'er ye worry, Thane," the midwife Bridie reassured him. "M'lady simply broke her water and she is ready for the birthing, 'tis all. Sit ye down here and wait and before the night is o'er, a new Da' ye will be. This I promise!"

He waited for hours in a large chair by the fire, his body comfortable enough, but his mind unnerved and emotionally distressed by the uncertainty of the night's eventual conclusion. The platter on the adjacent table overflowed with fruit, cheese, and bread, but concern for his child's welfare outweighed his need for food or rest. His nerves frayed and his wife's muted cries, although barely audible where he sat by the warm and crackling fire, enlisted a profound uneasiness in their nervous listener.

Like an insidious vapor, the sounds of her difficult labor wafted through the air, searching meticulously for a crack or crevice in the thick stone walls through which to pass. The obstinate sound waves groped the impervious granite as the tenacious hands of a blind man, finally discovering a painstakingly sought after egress, not through the impenetrable stone, but instead around the edges of the sturdy wooden door that separated the bedroom from the sitting room. No stranger to physical battle, Rhys faced a greater challenger in this intangible, invisible auditory enemy which threw him off-kilter. The intensity of her vocal labor stabbed him with a thousand vengeful daggers, cast from the very depths of the Underworld by Hades himself. With the bravado of an exhausted swordsman, he attempted to deflect each of Mahrea's moans and shouts, but appallingly unable to deflect the unrelenting parry of her periodic outbursts.

When Bridie's spindly arms pushed the heavy door open, he felt an immediate sense of relief. *Good news or bad, it matters not,* he thought. Until now, he engaged blindly in a figurative hand-to-hand combat with a ghostly and elusive enemy. As a soldier and a warlord, he much rather face a tangible opponent where the uncertainty of this psychological battle materializes into a concrete and more manageable adversary.

The midwife reminded him of an industrious and pragmatic spider with her bony arms and legs: fragile, nimble attachments to her box-like and diminutive torso. Her bulging eyes, ringed with dark circles of fatigue, gazed furtively at Rhys underneath pencil-thin eyebrows. In the flickering firelight, they resembled the compound eyes of a diligent and conscientious arthropod. *Half-human, half-insect*, he thought to himself. *Perhaps she was transformed into this hideous yet amusing chimera by some evil witch's enchantment?* he laughingly thought to himself as he allowed this ludicrous and entertaining mental image to materialize in his slightly delirious imagination.

The creature spoke. "It will be soon now, my Laird," she declared. "The child's crown is at m'Lady's entrance and her pains are now more frequent."

She paused and met not his eye. She studied the carpet in a poorly concealed and contrived effort to delay the necessary continuation of their conversation. *She is fearful for some reason, but not because she has bad news to convey*, he hurriedly concluded. Her nervous demeanor seemed awkward, which kept more with a servant faced with the delicate and uncomfortable task of delivering an unsavory message to her Lord.

"Go on, Bridie," he urged with kindness in his voice. "You are only the messenger, so say what you intend freely and without fear of reprisal."

She took in a long breath. "She asks for you to take your leave, Master, so the sounds of her final efforts are made with some degree of modesty and privacy."

Bridie was visibly startled by his laughter. "'Tis all, Midwife?" he asked with a smile. "I will gladly honor my wife's request, Bridie. Go tend to her, please and assure her I will not hear."

***

Shortly thereafter, he gratefully left the confining walls of the small antechamber and found himself wandering the cold and damp corridors of his sprawling castle. He drifted as a smug sleepwalker, who secretly escaped from a restless downy prison. No longer confined to his bed of ennui, he stretched his legs of freedom as he meandered aimlessly through the deserted maze of tunnels. His shadow, a flickering and distorted shape on the torch-lit walls, seemed to eerily mirror his dazed and bleary sleep-deprived consciousness. Although he knew where he roamed, he was in no apparent rush to reach his chosen destination. The fatigue and stress of the last twelve hours bore heavily on him and his pace uncharacteristically unhurried.

Finally, he arrived at the spiraling staircase. He began the ascent to his sanctuary in the highest castle tower, his boot-clad footsteps echoed in the dizzying cylinder of the tower stairwell. The hypnotic rhythm served to enhance the trance-like journey he made with slow deliberation to the tower's summit. One hundred and ninety-nine steps later, he reached the small room where he spent many hours in pensive thought and private meditation.

The sparsely-furnished, comfortable, circular room was illuminated by a dozen flaming candles, which by his order were never extinguished and continuously replenished. A small, but contented cot adorned the far wall, while a desk and chair decorated the adjacent rim of the curving wall. His journal lay open on the desk, waiting patiently for the next installment from its thoughtful owner. A large fireplace stacked with wood remained unlit. He shivered in the cold. Briskly, he pushed open the double doors that led him onto the small tower balcony, upon which he now stood.

A strong frigid breeze blew on his face and through his dark brown hair as a welcomed antidote to his languor and fatigue. He rested his strong arms on the icy stone ledge, warmed his hands on one another. His breath, a swirling white mist, exhaled over his hands and fingers, the smoky envelope of each expired breath tangible for only a brief moment, fleeting and transient in its conception, the symbolic representation of a mortal lifetime. *Ephemeral and temporary, like the human fate we all share*, he thought quietly to himself.

The ordeal taking place in Mahrea's bedroom now seemed miles and ages away. *But a child!* He thought happily about the symbol of immortality and permanence, conceived from his own flesh and blood and a vehicle to carry his legacy beyond the boundaries of his own lifetime. Perhaps his son or his daughter delivers him from the sadness and regret surrounding his marriage to the icy and fiery-haired Mahrea.

He pondered the events leading up to his wedding last spring. His union with Mahrea amounted to nothing more than a most regrettable necessity and obligation of duress conceived and executed by Olaf the Red, King of Mann and the Isles. His sole intent for the marriage meant to strengthen political ties between the Gaels and the Vikings. Rhys gave up so much of himself by relenting to Olaf's convincing and malicious coercion, resulting in a most unfortunate marital predicament. He sighed. *Perhaps this baby will fill the gaping emptiness*, he thought. He would soon learn if his child, who was likely entering the world at this very moment, would fill the cavernous void in his chest.

Dunscaith, his massive castle, perched on a rocky precipice built atop the precipitous slope of a ragged sea cliff which jutted like a small peninsula to meet the pounding surf of the Skye coastline. The full moon and the night were cold and breezy. Drifting tendrils of grey clouds floated like weary and defeated soldiers, who trudged slowly across an eerie celestial battlefield on a melancholy journey home. The translucent slate-colored warriors, exhausted, wounded and disenchanted after some fruitless supernatural conflict, occasionally paused for a brief respite on Diana's pale and naked navel as a heavier cloud cover settled on the moon goddess's lunar body draping her in a dark but transparent silk camisole. The covering obscured, but never completely eliminated the glowing brilliance of her heavenly nudity.

Rhys smiled as he stood on a small terrace that protruded from the peak of the soaring tower. He noticed the dark outline of a feathery visitor perched on the stone railing to the left. The osprey made the tower her home. She tended to her hatchlings for the past three seasons in a large nest she built on an exterior drainage ledge, five or six feet below the outer edge of the circular parapet. He called to her softly, hoping she moved closer to grace him with her company. "Kira," he beckoned, using the name he gave her years before, "come to me now."

She looked at him briefly; her black eyes glittered in the soft moonlight, before she dove majestically from the railing into the blackness below, her wings flapped noiselessly as she decisively declined his invitation. He laughed gently as he leaned out over the incomplete darkness stretched endlessly to the left of the tower's balcony, watched with happy envy as the beautiful bird of prey flaunted her glorious freedom. "Return soon, Friend," he said, wishing he too could escape the prison of his castle, if only for a moment and join her in happy flight.

As he leaned forward over the battlement, the impact of the altitude suddenly registered in all five of his senses with a dizzying rush. He stepped back from the ledge for fear he might lose his balance and topple from the castle's pinnacle to his death on the rocks below. The whitecaps were distant shimmering lines of undulating pallor, and his eyes saw them in a fleeting illusion as an army of brilliant white serpents. They rode the waves in grotesque and orderly formation, advancing towards an invisible and sand-obscured opponent with relentless and untiring resolve. From the tower's peak, the remote sound of the waves reached his ears like the delicate and tender whisper of a lover. Their hushed proposition bewitched and entranced, like the soft and beseeching call of the dark-haired beauty constantly haunting his dreams. The taste and smell of the salty sea diluted by the cold odorless wind blew from the nearby mountains and the harsh tactile sting of the winter breeze reminded him of the chilly weather top on his towering fortress, owned much more in common with the climate's upper atmosphere.

He stood with his arms crossed and the candlelight coming from the room behind him cast his wavering shadow onto the stone floor of the balcony. The chilly wind reached into the room and played with each candle flame like a cat toying with a mouse. The invisible paws batted the burning wicks back and forth causing his shadowy apparition to sway and undulate eerily on the smooth, broad table of granite in front of him. His dark silhouette mirrored his own melancholy spirit with its rippling movements pleading for reunion with its parent soul residing deep within his body's vessel.

Lost in these thoughts, Rhys failed to register the heavy and tenuous footsteps as they approached across the carpeted floor of the tower room onto the adjacent stone surface of the balcony terrace. Ironically, he only noticed the sound of the grave leather boots after their owner stopped short a few paces behind him. The silence of this portentous pause awoke him from his dreamy and philosophical reverie.

He felt the heavy weight of hesitation would shortly fall onto his broad shoulders and crush him like a tiny insect. The broad shadow of the messenger stood silently behind him, blocking the candlelight with his massive body and casting a bleak, suffocating shadow onto the balcony ledge.

"Well?" he said, without turning. He feared the words about to reach his ears.

"Rhys," the voice replied, "I bring news of your Lady's labor." It was Caedmon, his first lieutenant and his closest friend.

Rhys MacAulaed turned slowly to face his friend. He knew Caedmon's chosen task as the fateful courtier and bearer of news concerning Mahrea's labor.

"You knew where to find me, dear friend," Rhys said softly.

"Of course, my Lord," Caedmon replied, his tone straightforward and respectful. "Of late, you have been spending hours at a stretch in your tower. When I did not find you asleep in your bedchamber, I knew where my search would lead me next."

The Thane of Skye pulled back his shoulders and took a step closer to his friend. His voice was strong and steady as he braced himself to hear Fate's verdict.

"Tell me, Caedmon," he asked, "do you bring me good news, or bad?"

"I fear there is bad news to tell... along with the good," Caedmon responded.

Rhys took in a breath. "Out with it, Man. Am I a father? A simple yea or nay will suffice."

"You are indeed a father, my Liege," Caedmon said. "Your Lady hath born you a healthy and vigorous baby girl and she is indeed a beautiful sight!"

Rhys breathed a sigh of relief. "And Mahrea?" he asked, almost as an afterthought, given his resigned indifference to their tepid marriage. "Is she well or were there difficulties and complications you come to tell?"

"Mahrea is well, my Lord," Caedmon hesitated, his voice hushed and his lips trembling.

"If you have more to tell, Caedmon, please do so without further hesitation," he prompted, sincerely puzzled by his friend's distress. *If my child and Mahrea are both well, what could possibly be troubling him so?*

Caedmon looked down. "She bore a second child, Rhys. He came as a surprise, shortly after the girl was delivered."

"And?" Rhys asked, knowing in advance the answer to his question.

"Stillborn, my Liege," Caedmon said with regret in his voice. "A son, but he ne'er breathed a single breath in this world. The Lady's cord twisted around his precious neck."

Rhys staggered backward a step, overcome momentarily with the shock of this brutal news. Mahrea carried low and large, but none guessed twins grew in her pregnant womb.

His son, whom he would have raised as his heir and successor whom he would have loved with his fullest heart and deepest soul - his son, who someday might ascend to become a warrior king. His son, who died before breathing a single breath. What a sad and tragic premature ending to a life extinguished before it even began, a candlewick drenched with tears instead of oil. The strongest spark or flame never to ignite his candle now and it remains cold and lifeless like the frigid winter's night hosting his unnatural and bitter demise.

But I have a daughter, he thought happily. A healthy and beautiful baby warmed now by the heat of her mother's bosom and the promise of her father's love. His heart pounded with excitement. She would be his special child, the daughter who effortlessly sidestepped the hand of Death, succeeding in triumph where her unfortunate twin brother fought valiantly but failed. Their twin souls, in a single body share one destiny for two beings. Her destiny was to become the Mistress of Skye, the beloved Princess of the Isles, and Queen Scathach's legendary heir. He would name her Niamh; she would be the bright light in his shadowy fortress and a radiant shaft of hope for the entire kingdom.

A light flurry of snow now fell, signaling a gentle sign of hope and a silent harbinger of joy. The soft flakes fluttered gently on the balcony railing, a blessing descended from the heavens.

"I must see her, Caedmon," he insisted with excitement. "Take me to my daughter, who I shall call Niamh, which means 'bright'. She will be my hope, and this entire kingdom's brilliant light."

Caedmon nodded his acknowledgment, but said nothing. *Is there something more he hesitates to disclose?*

Rhys looked carefully at his friend's face, which looked uncharacteristically expressionless. *Yes, there is something more amiss that he does not share*, Rhys concluded.

He grasped Caedmon firmly with both hands on his shoulders and the mere proximity forced his friend to meet his intense hazel gaze.

"If there is more to tell, Caedmon, I pray you do so," he demanded.

His lieutenant turned his gaze downward. "You will see, Rhys," he said. "Come with me now, please."

Caedmon gently but firmly disengaged his general's grip. He turned away, walked brusquely into the balcony room and towards the spiraling dark staircase, leaving Rhys no choice but to follow. They descended silently into the cavernous and yawning abyss of the endless stairwell.

The powerful Lord of Skye felt helpless. And although he wasn't entirely sure what awaited him in the dreaded bedchamber below, he knew whatever it was would change his life forever.

Chapter Two
Nursemaid

Rhys, who followed closely behind Caedmon, stepped from the rejuvenating chill of the corridor into the warmth of the bedroom antechamber. The burning logs in the fireplace created a stifling atmosphere in the small room, which brought to mind an unwholesome raging fever in a sickly invalid. The air, dense with heat, parted like a curtain when the winter air pursued them into the room through the open door.

The oppression of the anaemic stale air in the chamber bore down on him. The transfusion of air promised to sweep inward from the castle corridor. Like a wise and experienced physician tending to an enigmatic patient, he quickly recognized the proper treatment to alleviate the suffocating cloud of repression threatening to strangle and choke. He left the door open to its full extent. The cold draft was a potent inoculation propelled from the syringe of the hallway into the ailing antechamber with a triumphant rush of welcome resuscitation.

The landscape of the room changed radically during his brief interlude on the tower balcony. Three slim attendants stood motionless in the shadowy periphery, as if preserved remnants of tree trunks guarding the secrets of an ancient and lifeless petrified forest. Rhys could not distinguish their features shrouded in the sweeping drape of darkness that cloaked the edges and corners of the chamber. Bridie stood in front of the fireplace as still as a solitary stone monolith in a crumbing druid ritual site. In her arms she held her pagan sacrifice to transfer from the granite altar of her cradling embrace into God's loving protection. The child's body concealed in a thin, white blanket. *He is as still and cold as a piece of marble*, Rhys thought with a shudder.

The shadows symbolized macabre actors performing a tragedy on the rough stone walls as they danced grotesquely in the pulsing firelight. As he took in the scene portrayed in the bedroom suite, a peculiar black shape on the chair by the fireplace caught his eye. *Is this simply a distorted shadow cast from the crooked pillar of Bridie's looming form or perchance a new character in the drama unfolding before me?* he asked. The dark shape moved and then leapt from the chair to cross the room directly in front of Rhys's path.

Ciara, Mahrea's pitch black feline, he realized, unable to suppress the brief jolt of fear he always felt when he encountered his wife's familiar. He crossed himself, superstitiously invoking the protection of his God against the unholy animal. She crossed the room, settled herself on her haunches outside the bedroom door like Cerberus guarding the gates of hell. Her emerald eyes sent a silent warning as they peered intently at Rhys through shifting and sentient slits. *The price to enter might be my soul*, he imagined with a silent laugh accompanied by a sobering quiver of dread.

He noticed with surprise one of the servants, who stood deferentially in the shadows, held a parcel that kicked and moved with the joyful signs of life. He furrowed his brow, trying to understand why the baby suckling not with Mahrea. Then, in a flash, he understood Caedmon's unspoken forewarning something was amiss.

She wants not her child, he thought. *Surely this must be the only explanation for this unnatural separation of new-born child from mother*.

He shook off his surprise and concern, pleasantly distracted by the miraculous new arrival that squirmed in her caretaker's arms. It seemed as if he watched a drama laid out on a stage before him, whose scene changed abruptly due to the introduction of a new character. In an instant, the room transformed, in his mind's eye, from a cursed enchanted wood into a green and blessed meadow - all because of one tiny infant. The beauty of his new perspective gave him hope the drama of his own life might not end in tragedy, after all.

He started towards his daughter, who squirmed in the servant's slender and youthful arms, but then, he thought again and turned instead toward Bridie. He knew he must first gaze upon the face of his infant son and bid him farewell before he greeted his living heir. He owed him this much, at least, to the memory of the child who would, sadly, never grow into a boy or a man. Although his heart pained him to, he approached the midwife.

Lifting the blanket covering his son's face, Rhys gazed sorrowfully at the tiny motionless features of his stillborn child. *So peaceful*, he thought. *No pain here, only the regret and remorse of a life that would never be*. He gently stroked the baby's cheek, which felt soft but cold. The tears welled in his eyes blurred his vision and he twisted away. Wiping the tears from his cheek, he motioned despondently to the midwife, indicating he saw enough.

Bridie bowed, covered the boy's face again with the blanket. She turned to leave, but Rhys thought twice about her abrupt dismissal. As she passed, he laid a kind and gentle hand on her arm to stop her.

"My thanks to you, Midwife, for your talents and knowledge," he spoke. "There was naught you could do about the boy, Woman. There is no blame here, Bridie, just forgiveness and thanks. I pray you should know this."

She nodded. "Ye be kind and gracious, m'Laird. I am yer true and faithful servant."

One of the servants emerged from the shadows, took the motionless body from the midwife's trembling arms. Overcome with emotion and exhaustion, she dropped to the floor, her body shook with intense sobs.

Rhys knelt down beside her. "I share your grief, Woman," he said, "And know your sorrow because it is my own."

He kindly grasped her bony shoulders, helping her up. Looking in her eyes, he searched carefully for answers to his next.

She seemed to know his mind. "She wants not the girl, m'Laird," she whispered in a confidential tone laced with panic and concern. "She sent me out with the sweet child and told me ne'er to return with her."

He nodded, his fears confirmed. "Since my daughter is with your attendant instead of in the bedchamber suckling at her mother's breast, I expected this unnatural news. This muted disclosure from your weary lips brings me sorrow, but no surprise."

She looked down. "I am sorry, m'Liege. Gave her the babe to nurse, did I, but she pushed the sweet child away with violent anger."

"Worry not, Bridie, I will handle her. Go now to your well-deserved rest. You are dismissed, Midwife."

"Me thanks, m'Laird," she said, grateful for his kindness. She wiped her red and bloodshot eyes - as much from fatigue as from her recent weeping. "May God be with you and with m'Lady." She bowed a final time, leaving the room accompanied by two of the servants, one of whom still held the stillborn prince.

Caedmon, assumed a deferential position by the doorway, shifted restlessly where he stood. He cleared his throat to get Rhys' attention, while at the same time glanced nervously in the direction of the servant who held Niamh.

"Thane," he said with a troubled frown, "I ask your permission to assist with preparations for the stillborn child." He looked again at the attendant who stood in the shadows in the corner.

Rhys studied his lieutenant with curiosity. *What troubles him now?* Rhys thought. *Could there be more, yet, that I still do not know?* he wondered, unable to decipher Caedmon's uneasiness. He glanced swiftly from his friend to the servant and back, but unable to perceive anything amiss in either of their appearances.

Rhys shrugged. "You are dismissed, Caedmon," he said. "Tend to my unfortunate son and then get some sleep, my friend."

"Thank you, Liege," Caedmon replied. As he bowed, he looked once more towards the corner of the room before he turned on his heel and took his leave.

***

Rhys was now alone with the nursemaid who held his new-born daughter. She stood calmly and silently in the shadows, her features obscured in the darkness.

Momentarily, he realized she waited for him to give his next command. He cleared his throat. "Approach now, Woman" he said bluntly, "so I may see my child and meet the servant who is attending her."

After a brief moment of hesitation, the attendant stepped forward into the light. The candles, which burned softly on the mantle of the fireplace, threw a gentle yellow illumination onto her beautiful face. Her dark walnut hair pulled back away from her face, dangled like slender willow branches onto the cream-colored pools of both of her smooth shoulders. Her violet eyes reflected the orange embers of the dying fire. She gazed at Rhys with a boldness he remembered well.

The abrupt and unexpected disclosure of her identity hit him with physical intensity, causing him to react with an involuntary and audible gasp. "My sweet God," he whispered, stunned by the unbelievable vision before him. She was a specter he never expected to see again, but there she stood before him. His own Persephone, who miraculously emerged from the Underworld after her rescue by

Hermes. *She is the reason Caedmon seemed so ill at ease!* he told himself, stunned and elated by this unexpected yet wonderful turn of events.

Sweet Gwenhwyvar, my one and only! he thought, as if the mental confirmation of her identity somehow brought finality and permanence to her startling return. Their goodbye two and a half years ago, poignant and sorrowful, failed to grant either of them closure. He often prayed for reconciliation, but with time he grudgingly resigned himself to the unsatisfying manner in which their relationship ended. Yet, here she was before him as if conjured to appear by a necromancer's spell.

She materialized in a similar fashion at the welcoming banquet a year and a half ago, when Mahrea first arrived at the castle as his new wife. She had somehow been enlisted as one of the servers, attempting to cloak her true identity by lightening her hair and darkening her skin. Despite her attempt to disguise her appearance, he recognized her immediately. For, after all, her eyes gave her away! Her deep blue gaze swept across the room with the force of a rampant tempest, ripping through his entire being like a violent windstorm. The raging wind of her presence in the room swirled around him, stripped him naked and left him vulnerable and helpless in the face of the unexpected emotional assault. Oh, how he wished the storm of her sexuality would ravage and devastate his lovesick body again. As he stared at her from across the banquet hall, he imagined the feel of her naked body pressed against his - knowing he would never feel that pleasure again, given the binding and cursed promises he made to a woman he did not know and could never love.

With no opportunity to draw her away for a private discussion during the celebrations, he searched for her afterwards, his heart filled with the hope of a possible brief reunion. Alas, his hopes cruelly dashed as he scoured the empty corridors, his joy scattered like a thousand shards of glass on the floor of his disappointment. She disappeared, without a single word of explanation or a second glance his way. Heartbroken by her apparent rejection, he abandoned all hopes of ever seeing her again, yet here she was, as radiant and as beautiful as he remembered from their halcyon days together.

"Gwen," he stammered, temporarily rendered inarticulate by the overwhelming potency of his emotions.

She bowed her head, holding the baby close to her breast as she gave a slight curtsy. When she looked at him again, he noticed the tears in her eyes.

"I am indeed your humble and simple servant, m'Lord," she said, her voiced laced with sadness and more than a touch of sarcasm. She raised her head high; the gesture in itself portrayed an intentional and pointed contradiction to the self-deprecating reference regarding her lowly social status. Her eyes, though still moist with tears, burned with the intense reminder of their past together. They never were social equals, but their intensely physical and passionate romance somehow adjusted or even reversed this discrepancy. Consumed in the ecstasy of their romance, he often felt she was the all-powerful ruler and he the helpless knave - tempted and seduced, always and without exception, by the irresistible command of her supreme desire. The recollection of these memorable nights from so long ago made her cynical verbal retort sting as if she slapped him in the face.

His remorse and guilt, although by no means insignificant, were pale dwarf stars compared to the radiating red giant of his joy and excitement she returned. His heart pounded with aching exhilaration as he imagined the possibility his prayers answered. She plagued his thoughts and haunted his dreams every single day since their last goodbye and he secretly hoped for a physical and emotional reunion. *Perhaps now I can finally make amends for our past.*

"I am overjoyed to see you, Gwen. How are you, sweet woman?" he asked. Rapidly recovering his composure, he took two steps forward to greet her. He reached out to touch her arm, his face beaming and his cock aching as his skin touched hers.

"I am well, Rhys." Her cheeks, flushed red with self-conscious smooth rose-tinted alabaster color. She smoothed some strands of loose brown hair away from her face with her free hand, as if the effort might somehow distract from her embarrassment.

Rhys looked fondly on his former lover, remembering well how soft her skin felt under his fingertips and how her silken hair smelled like the fresh wind blowing across a field of wheat. He smiled broadly, hoping he could put her at ease with his innate and unaffected kindness, as he used to, years ago.

"My sweet Gwen," he said, "so much time passed since our last meeting. Pray, tell me how you have fared and also how you arrived here in such an unlikely capacity."

She returned his smile, her enticing lips full and red like a silky rose petal and her seductive eyes a deep, inviting shade of indigo purple.

"I have been well, my Lord," she replied, moistening her lips with her tongue while she wore an unconvincing expression of innocence on her lovely face.

He interrupted her with a gesture. "We have known each other in the most intimate of ways, Gwen. There are no false pretenses between us. You may call me Rhys when we speak in private, as we are doing now."

She nodded her thanks. "My dear Rhys," she started, pausing for a moment in an undisguised attempt to collect her thoughts. "I became pregnant shortly after your wedding nuptials," she explained with a sigh, "and my own child is now six months old. My breasts are still full and eager, as you can see," she said, drawing his attention to her full and swollen breasts by briefly cupping one of them suggestively with her free hand, "but my son no longer requires the nourishment my fruitful bosom can still provide. It would please me to serve you and my mistress by offering my milk to your child, if you and God are willing to accept my gift."

His heart sank when he heard her words. *She has a child. Surely she has forgotten me, then, if a husband she has taken*. The finality of this foregone conclusion seemed to dash his unrealistic fantasies of their happy reconciliation and reunion.

Well why should she not marry? he reasoned, in a half-hearted attempt to lesson his disappointment with rational logic. *It was my actions that betrayed our love after all,* he reminded himself sadly. There would be no conceivable reason for her to sacrifice her own happiness by remaining single, especially when he seemingly tossed aside her love to marry another.

Her breasts were indeed large and ripe. His cock strained against his leggings, as he recalled with poignant melancholy the many long and passionate nights they enjoyed together as lovers. He knew her naked body well and it was not very difficult to undress her in his mind now as he gazed upon her unmatched, tantalizing sensuality and beauty.

He first bedded her years ago, with the burning fire of lusty desire in his heart, but he soon learned their unique connection went well beyond the physical. Her carnal enthusiasm as well as her capacity to give freely of her deepest soul and spirit matched or exceeded his own, he recalled with a pang of tender remorse. During their twelve-month affair which satisfied their mutual hunger for sexual and emotional intimacy, he had been happier than he ever imagined possible.

She is as beautiful and physically compelling as ever, he thought sadly as he gazed longingly at her seductive curves and scantily covered breasts. *She must be twenty or twenty-one years old now*, he reflected. The years made no mark on her youthful body which looked no different now than when he first met her three years earlier.

"You are beautiful still, Gwen," he commented. "Your pregnancy left your youthful curves untouched. You are absolutely stunning," he said.

His honest compliment made her blush. She smiled, reached out with one hand to touch his arm. "You are kind, Rhys." She paused. "You too, changed very little since we last met. The years passed slowly for me, without you, but they left no visible mark on your handsome face." She looked at him questioningly, apparently unsure if she should continue as she planned.

"Go on, Gwen," he prompted. He was jolted by her words.

"I have missed you, Rhys," she confessed with down-turned eyes.

His heart and his mind raced, as he processed the implications of her words. *I have missed her, too*, he thought, as he pictured in his mind's eye the soft curves of her naked body lying beneath him in the throes of passion. They shared a unique physical and emotional closeness he never and would never share with any other partner, for the rest of his days. His ten-inch cock, now fully aroused, screamed for that intimacy, especially since Mahrea rejected any and all advances from her husband these past nine months. Ever since she became pregnant, Mahrea insisted they sleep in separate bedchambers, claiming the well-being of their baby demanded she remain untouched for the entire duration of her term.

He tried to suppress his sexual excitement, knowing full well Gwen might not share his premature willingness to revisit the intimacy of their shared past. *Caution!* he warned, realizing further exploration of their feelings for each other should wait for a more opportune moment. *There will be ample time and opportunity for explanations later, if she remains at Dunscaith as a nursemaid for Niamh,* he mused as he made a decision to divert their conversation into safer waters.

"How is your father?" he asked, hoping she would not misinterpret his failure to acknowledge her attempt to bare her soul. He remembered Bryon's kindness and hospitality that night three years ago, which indirectly and inadvertently encouraged the physical intimacy Rhys enjoyed with the uninhibited and sensual farmer's daughter.

She nodded, acknowledging and understanding his hesitation as if she read his mind. "He suffers from rheumatism," she replied in a matter of fact tone, "especially when the weather is cold as it has been this past fortnight. But otherwise, he manages well."

He smiled warmly and looked lovingly into the depths of her rich mauve eyes. "You are, of course, welcome in my service, sweet damsel," he said. "My wife will welcome you as well, I am quite sure."

He paused to reflect briefly on this last comment, which he articulated sincerely but without thinking. Would Mahrea actually allow his former lover to nurse and care for her baby without protest? Unlikely, unless she remained oblivious to the past he shared with the beautiful daughter of one of his serfs.

He found himself engaged in a conversation. *My past with Gwen should not be very difficult to conceal,* he replied to his inner self, *since, after all, our romance was always a safely guarded secret.* He carefully reviewed the circumstances surrounding their clandestine romance, by necessity remained intensely private. Gwen was a peasant, and Rhys, the powerful Lord of Skye, although this class discrepancy became less and less important as their relationship matured, the unlikelihood of a legal union between a thane and a serf's daughter imposed a cautious approach to their romance from the start. If they would never lie together as man and wife, due to the social conventions of the day, he did not want to sabotage her chances to build a life with another man by flaunting their frequent, enjoyable sexual indiscretions. In order to protect Gwen's virginal reputation, the covert trysts and furtive rendezvous known to no one except for Caedmon. On many occasions, Rhys's loyal friend and lieutenant escorted the cloaked and concealed maiden in the dead of night on horseback, without creating the slightest suspicion, to arrive at Rhys's royal quarters without being seen or recognized by anyone.

    He laughed to himself at the irony. After twelve months of frustrating vigilance, he was on the verge of asking for her hand in marriage. Indeed, it was a bold move for him to disregard the convention of the day by marrying a woman of lowly birth, but he had no choice in the matter. Quite simply, he fell deeply and completely in love with her and the pull utterly irresistible. She was the magnet that effortlessly retracted the iron nails from the hinges of his rationale mind and the doorway to his soul was now wide open.

But alas, Olaf's ambitions thwarted his plans. King of the Isles abruptly called him away to meet privately at his castle on Mann and when Rhys returned to Skye, he grudgingly belonged to another woman. Humiliated and defeated, unable to face her after being strong-armed by Olaf into accepting the politically motivated pairing. He sorely regretted the cowardly manner in which he ended his relationship with his one true love, but worse yet, Gwen never knew he intended to make her his wife.

Rhys recalled his fateful meeting with the self-serving Olaf, known disparagingly as "Morsel" to many in the island kingdom. The nickname referred to Olaf's shameless eagerness to exploit each and every opportunity to consolidate his power - no matter how small the morsel. The name also referred to his excessive frugality, bordering on the obsessive, especially as it pertained to food. Rhys heard on one occasion, Morsel ordered a servant's execution for feeding some perfectly good leftovers to the cook's hounds.

The Thane watched with curiosity from the other side of the table, as Morsel inspected a massive turkey drumstick he held in his hand. Although he already meticulously picked the last shred of meat from the bone, Olaf appeared to search for any remnants that might have escaped his thorough gastronomic attentions. Finally satisfied the avian limb devoid of edible flesh, he tossed the bone with content nonchalance over his shoulder, reaching at the same moment for new quarry.

He was not prepared to attack his second helping just yet. Laying it on the table in front of him, he looked thoughtfully at Rhys as if he appraised an opponent immediately prior to hand-to-hand combat. His hearty belch resonated in the empty hall, like a preamble to his forthcoming soliloquy, the contents of which Rhys, unfortunately, been unable to determine in advance.

Morsel cleared his throat. "I have promised my daughter Raignailt to the Thane of Kinn Tyre," he announced decisively, sounding as if he just now made the decision and needed Rhys' approval before he sent out the wedding invitations.

Rhys waited for the king to continue, but instead, Morsel picked up the second drumstick and preoccupied with the task in hand.

It is out of character for Olaf to share any aspect of his personal life with his warlords, Rhys thought, frowning. Even if he were a friend or a confidante to the King of the Isles, as he certainly was not, he could not believe this seemingly irrelevant disclosure the reason for the private conference requiring his urgent summoning and current attendance.

After a moment of silence, Rhys decided Morsel needed prompting to continue. "Somerled?" he asked, hoping mentioning the Thane's given name instigates a comment or two from the Viking, who ripped the flesh from the turkey bone with his teeth.

Rhys knew Somerled and respected him. A Gael with a trickle of Viking blood in his veins, Somerled proved himself at Olaf's side, along with Rhys in many a bloody battle. They were contemporaries, he and the Thane of Kinn Tyre in every sense of the word. Both in their early thirties, essentially warrior prodigies: youthful warlords who had both gained the respect of the Viking king as well as the love of the people of the Isles at an unprecedented early age.

They share more in common than political success. Equally handsome and good-natured, both sought after bachelors with countless suitors and a plentiful cadre of eager and lusty maidens to choose from. They both loathed conventional class distinctions and shared a love for the common people and the freedom of the open road. In fact, both Somerled and Rhys were well known for their wanderlust and both often enjoyed disguised and protracted adventures in the countryside during which they secretly learned the true sentiments and opinions of their loyal subjects.

Somerled, although outwardly loyal to his liege, had a private agenda he shared with Rhys on several occasions. Somerled, like Olaf, was an ambitious visionary, but unlike the currently seated King of Mann, Somerled's visions motivated by unselfishness. Somerled's desire to expand his prerogative in the Gaelic territories arose strictly from his love for the common people. Somerled's subjects, in turn, adored him, which is why Rhys was puzzled Olaf would promise his only daughter to such a popular competitor.

Morsel finished the drumstick. Wiping the grease from his hands on his beard, he nodded. "Yes indeed, Somerled," he replied. "What think you of this union, Rhys?"

Shrugging, Rhys met Morsel's look with suspicion. "It matters not what I think, my Liege."

"Ah, but it does," the king replied. "You are a most powerful Gael, not unlike your compatriot and friend. I would welcome your blessing and approval, my loyal Thane of Skye, in this union between Gael and Viking."

Rhys realized perhaps Olaf considered several matches for his daughter before deciding on Somerled and him on the short list. He breathed a sigh of relief. Thinking of Gwen, he thanked sweet God in heaven, Olaf selected Somerled instead.

Rhys smiled, nodding politely to Morsel from across the table. "I am honored you seek my opinion, my Lord. Somerled is the fortunate one in this engagement, my King. Your daughter is beautiful and the match will please this entire kingdom."

Morsel smiled deviously. "I am glad you approve, Rhys. The blending of Gael and Viking blood will make a new breed: strong, obstinate, and quite unwilling to bend to the will of a foreign master."

Rhys cocked his head, wondering where the conversation would lead next. *He is dangerous and fanatical!* He waited for further explanations from the ambitious king.

Olaf rose, visibly excited by his vision of a master race of islanders who eventually recognize Olaf and his successors as the autonomous King of the Hebrides. "I will rule as a true king, Rhys," he said, "if my vision becomes reality. But to do this, my plan must move forward without haste."

"Your plan, my Liege?" Rhys asked with trepidation. Morsel's agenda for their meeting ostensibly involved more than the simple announcement of his daughter's engagement to Somerled.

Olaf's eyes blazed with a crazed intensity. "Yes, Rhys, I have promised you to a Viking princess whose beauty surpasses any woman in this kingdom or any other."

Rhys couldn't breathe. His mouth went dry and although he tried to speak, the words froze.

"But..." Rhys finally managed to say, before the king interrupted.

"No arguments, my dear thane," he said, the finality of the arrangement evident in his voice. "The preparations for your nuptials have been made." He paused, leering at Rhys from across the table, the threat of enforcement clearly visible on his face.

Rhys, now composed, leaned forward in his chair. "And if I refuse?" he asked with calm and quiet defiance.

Olaf laughed. "Yes, you may certainly refuse," he replied, "but it would be a pity if anything should happen to that beautiful peasant mistress of yours."

Rhys felt dizzy. *He knows about Gwen, now I am truly defeated*, he recited with panicked resignation.

Morsel snickered. "Yes, I know about her, Thane. You will marry the Viking princess or else your lover will pay with her life."

Rhys was defeated. In order to save Gwen, he must betray their love. That night, he wrote her a letter and his tragic fate sealed.

He sighed, his thoughts returning now to Mahrea. *She knows nothing of my past with Gwen*, he thought and he needed to make sure she remained oblivious of this knowledge. It certainly helped Mahrea isolated herself to such an extent even the boldest attendant felt intimidated in her presence. Even if one of the domestics somehow discovered Gwen once been Rhys' mistress, it seemed unlikely Mahrea would befriend a common servant to the extent they would share such confidences with each other.

Shaking himself back to reality, he realized Gwen spoke. "I simply hope she blesses and welcomes my service, Rhys," she quavered. "She would not keep the baby and the infant needs to be fed soon!" she said, the earnest apprehension apparent in the tone of her sweet voice.

"I am aware of this, lovely nursemaid," he said kindly. He hoped using the title would help reassure Gwen her commission at Dunscaith was undisputed, at least in his mind.

He glanced nonchalantly at her full breasts, barely covered with the thin material of her nursing garment. Her cleavage, a canyon between two mountainous hillsides, disappeared seductively under the loosely fitting cotton of her simple gown. *She is leaking milk*, he realized as he noticed the wetness darkening the front of her chemise. How he longed to feel her breasts again, pressed firmly against his muscular chest or resting urgently in the cradling cup of his needy hands. As he examined the evidence of her firm nipples straining against her scant bodice, he recalled with nostalgia how they hardened so readily under the soft caress of his fingertips, so many years ago.

She simply exudes sex, he thought, *just as she always has*. His desire for her seemed to boil in his veins. *Caution, Rhys*, he warned himself. He needed to exert a monumental effort to control the physical pull he felt towards her, he knew seemed as primal and carnal now as before when they were lovers.

Niamh cried with urgent need, rooting unsuccessfully against Gwen's heaving bosom. How ironic his former lover was now the nursemaid to his new-born daughter. Her deep violet eyes engaged his own hazel ones with an intensity that made him feel dizzy. So many questions in their depths, but he could only answer one of them now.

"Tend to her now, Maiden," he replied. "There is no need for modesty in my presence."

She sat on the chair, cradling the crying baby in her arms. With unashamed boldness, she loosened the interlacing string that secured the front of her nursing gown, pulling the two halves of the bodice apart and pushed the fabric downward to swiftly and openly bare her full bosom. To his delight and surprise, both of her round full breasts were now fully exposed. She glanced briefly at Rhys, undoubtedly in order to judge his response to her boldness.

She smiled at him with a subtle hint of testing provocation as she cupped her left teat in her palm and guided Niamh's hungry lips onto her dripping nipple. He glanced longingly at her other breast which became stimulated to let down her milk by the baby's efforts on the other side. Glistening streams of cloudy liquid dripped from her firm engorged nipple, trickling like tiny rivulets onto the mound of her areola and down the hillside of her luscious, tantalizing bosom. He imagined the taste of her milk on his tongue. He longed to lick from the beckoning swell of her engorged and bountiful nipples.

He looked away. His heart pounded. She uncovered herself in his presence intentionally, hoping her exposed sexuality re-ignited his lust for her perfect body and her pure soul. *She has desire for me still,* he thought. Perhaps she came to Dunscaith not only to offer her services to his child, but also to rekindle their romance. *Nonsense*, he justified. *She is married and has a child with another man.* Nevertheless, her blatantly flirtatious behavior during their brief reunion could not be ignored. He needed to wade slowly and cautiously into these very dangerous waters.

He put these distracting thoughts out of his mind as he repositioned himself behind the chair so her breasts were partially concealed from his view. He laid one hand on Gwen's shoulder and the other on his daughter's head. The baby fed vigorously from the nursemaid's voluptuous teat. Gwen detached the child, swung her over to the right side to nurse from the other bosom.

"My dear Rhys, she is beautiful," Gwen whispered quietly. "I wish she was our child."

Again, her words hit him like a blow to the gut. She would never speak to him thus, if her intentions strictly professional. The regret in her voice truly surprised him. He assumed - incorrectly it seemed - she harbored bitter feelings towards him, after his impersonal and detached withdrawal from their relationship.

As he softly touched her hand, she squeezed his fingers with tender and loving pressure. The electricity of contact with her shot through him like a lightning bolt.

"Such a wish I might share with you, but wishing does not create a reality from which could never be," he replied softly and cautiously. His answer was intentionally non-committal. He required time to determine how to handle this unexpected turn of events.

Gwen nodded, seeming to understand his thoughts. *She always did have an uncanny ability to know my mind*, he reflected with a smile.

As the beautiful nursemaid gently and generously fed his new-born daughter, Rhys felt warm tears trickle down his cheek. His teardrops fell gently onto Niamh's tiny and precious downy crown and on Gwen's round and inviting shoulders and breasts.

He realized with some embarrassment he neglected to greet his new-born daughter. His tears flowed freely now as he smoothed his hand over her fragile head as she nursed. "I love you, sweet Niamh," he sobbed. *And I love you too, Gwen, with my whole heart and soul*, he added to himself. "Welcome to this world, my precious child. I am your father and we will know each other well, I pray."

"She is her father's daughter," Gwen commented. There was a touch of sadness in her voice. "She has your eyes, Rhys," she pointed out.

True, her eyes are hazel, he noticed. *Odd*, he thought. Most babies had blue eyes at first or so he had heard. *There is something wonderfully ancient and incredibly wise in those unusual and beautiful eyes*, he mused.

He gripped Gwen's hand tightly. "Yes, she is a special child... a kind and generous gift from God. I will treasure her and I know she will change my life."

His daughter, content and satiated, now lay dozing in Gwen's arms. He gently took her from the nursemaid, held her tightly against his chest and rubbed her back with his fatherly caress.

Gwen lifted her gown to cover her voluptuous breasts. She rose to her feet, touched Rhys' hands lightly as he held the new-born. "You will be good to her, Rhys, kind and tender, as you always were to me," she said, as she stepped a pace closer.

The tantalizing bulge of her generous bosom lightly touched Niamh's back. If he had not been holding his daughter, he could have easily pushed his body against hers to facilitate the physical contact he so missed and desired.

She was crying now. He wiped the tears from her eyes. "My sweet Gwen, we will talk later. You should know, Maiden, your arrival here makes me very happy indeed."

Smiling, she reached up and held the back of his head with both of her delicate hands. He did not resist. She pulled his head towards her waiting, wet lips anxious with her hot desire, closing his eyes; he felt the delicious and familiar touch of her probing tongue in his mouth.

She disengaged sooner than he liked. As she looked nervously at the door to Mahrea's bedchamber, he realized she was the cautious one now.

She stepped away from him. "Go now Rhys," she said. "Bring Niamh to her. Perhaps you will be able to reverse her fateful decision."

Nodding his agreement, he walked to the door. As he placed his hand on the cold iron doorknob, her final words sang in his ears like the celestial bells of heaven.

"I love you, Rhys," she said. "My heart is your captive and your servant it shall always be."

Chapter Three
Prophecy

Gwen watched nervously as Rhys disappeared into the uncertain darkness of his wife's private sanctuary. It seemed he was a courageous intruder venturing into dangerous and forbidden territory like an elite advance guard, exploring the well-secured position of some dreaded enemy with furtive and cautious determination. She looked after him wistfully, imagining in her daydream she walked by his side as he embarked on the impossible task that lay before him. She wished she could grasp his hand tightly as he faced his opponent, channelling the strength and power of her undying love from her body into his through her firm and committed grip. As he softly closed the door behind him, she saw Mahrea's black cat, an unlucky omen of impending disaster, slip into his bedroom.

She sat down on the edge of the chair, fully expecting him to emerge momentarily with Niamh still clutched to his broad chest. She possessed little hope for Rhys's success in his fruitless mission. Her keen feminine intuition knew his well-intentioned endeavor doomed to failure due to Mahrea's cold and corrupt heart. Gwen harbored no doubt the rumors true. She feared for Rhys's safety as he entered bravely into the fiery-haired witch's lair.

She knew it to be true from the moment she first gazed on Mahrea at the banquet a year and a half ago. Gwen changed her appearance using lemon juice and white vinegar to bleach her dark walnut hair and wolfberry extract to darken her smooth fair skin. After flattening her buxom chest with an uncomfortable and tightly drawn corset, she padded her slim and curvaceous hips with the bulge of a feather-filled waistband. She stayed far away from Rhys, for fear he recognize her and pull her aside to converse but despite this precaution, their gazes locked and she knew he quickly and easily unmasked her disguise. She fled the banquet, concerned that direct contact with her former lover would re-open the painful wounds so slow to heal.

Mahrea sat at Rhys's side, but despite the physical proximity to her new husband, she seemed isolated and emotionally removed from the bustling celebration. *She is beautiful*, Gwen thought, *but so very distant*. Her eyes were cold and she did not engage in conversation with Rhys or anyone else. She exuded an unnatural power which seemed to reach across the room, like an invisible claw threatening to strangle and scratch if provoked with the slightest degree of kindness. Gwen's inner spirit shuddered with the prospect of such contact and one brief glance into Mahrea's eyes filled her being with immediate fear and dread. Mahrea, a sorceress, trapped Rhys in her web of evil enchantment.

At that very moment, Gwen resolved to rescue Rhys from the binding spell, his wife cast upon him. The very next day, gathering a basket of eggs for payment, she visited Rhoswen, an old woman blessed with the gift of future seeing.

Rhoswen took the eggs with muttered thanks, placed them carefully on the shelf next to countless bottles and jars of herbs and remedies. She gathered two or three unmarked bottles, sifting a small amount of each into a large ceramic bowl. Pouring the entire amount of liquid from a heavy jug on the counter into the bowl, she carried the magical potion carefully in its basin and laid them carefully on the table in front of Gwen.

"Rest yer fingers in the seeing water, Lass," she crooned. "The potion will draw yer future into the liquid and I will tell ye what is reflected in the magic pond."

Gwen followed Rhoswen's demands. After a few moments her fingertips felt icy and numb in the tepid water. Her hands trembled as she felt a chilling surge of energy travel from her hands into her shoulders and back.

Gasping with alarm, she started to withdraw her hands. Rhoswen grasped her wrists - gently but firmly - to prevent her from breaking the contact presumably made with her future.

"The chill will pass, Child," she reassured. "Let me read yer future now, Lass."

Gwen relaxed and just as Rhoswen promised, the uncomfortable sensation in her arms gradually subsided.

Rhoswen looked into the water, passed her hands over the surface of the liquid to draw the images from the depths of the bowl and out of Gwen's psyche. Gwen studied Rhoswen's face, which become flat and expressionless. Her eyes stared trance-like into the calm surface of the potion. She seemed engaged in their task of observation and interpretation.

Finally, the old woman spoke. "I see a child," she said, "but she is not yours. You will care for her as if she were your own, but she belongs to another."

Rhoswen paused, gripped the edge of the bowl, and closed her eyes in a conscious effort to concentrate. "You have a son of your own, but he will be cared for willingly by your sister who understands what you must do."

Gwen's mouth felt dry. *Is this truly my future she reads?* she questioned. She had no husband and she remained virginal since Rhys left her over a year ago.

"Dear soothsayer," Gwen interrupted meekly, "I have taken no lovers, so how could this be?"

"The bowl does not lie," she said with conviction. "It has drawn yer future from yer digits, Lass and what I see will come to pass, as sure as the day is long."

"Go on then," Gwen urged. "I am prepared to hear more."

"Lie ye will, come the next full moon, with a passing minstrel most handsome. From his seed ye will bear a son."

She thought for a moment, taking in a breath to clear her mind. "My heart is promised elsewhere, Soothsayer," she explained. "I will never wed another," she proclaimed, the worry evident in her cracking voice.

Rhoswen laughed. "Worry not, Lass," she said, patting Gwen's knee with reassurance. "The gypsy will ne'er yer husband be, child. His cock ye will know but once and his wet desire will hit yer mother's mark." There was a twinkle in her eye. "Ne'er ye worry, Lass... the bard is not yer destiny."

Gwen breathed a sigh of relief. "And the second child?" she asked, curious to understand her predetermined future.

Rhoswen looked deeply into the water, seeming to ripple with subtle movement around each of Gwen's submerged fingertips. After a moment, she nodded as if she finally understood.

"She is the Laird's daughter," she concluded, confident now in her interpretation of the image. "The Mistress of Skye wants her not and you will be her nursemaid and Ma'."

Gwen's heart jumped into her throat. *Oh God in heaven*, she thought, *you answered my prayer, and I thank you from my deepest soul.*

"Is there more, Woman?" Gwen asked anxiously.

Rhoswen peered into the water, as if she looked through a window to the future. "Yes, Dearie," she concluded. "His mistress ye shall be again."

Gwen pulled her fingers from the water with abrupt excitement, accidentally overturning the bowl as she did so.

"Calm ye, child," Rhoswen chided as she reached for a rag to dry the spillage. "Ye must be cautious in this yer future, for I see danger as well as happiness in these prophesies."

Gwen pushed away her chair, unconcerned with the old woman's warnings. She reached across the table, warmly grasping the old woman's hands in hers in a gesture of heartfelt thanks.

"My dear Rhoswen," she bubbled. "You made me the happiest lass in all of Skye. Thank you, Soothsayer."

The old woman's eyes sparkled. She bowed her head slightly as if she offered deference to a lady of privilege and title. "And the Mistress of Skye ye shall surely be, m'Lady," she said softly.

Gwen looked at Rhoswen cautiously. "I know not whether you speak in jest and at my expense, Fortune Teller."

The seer shook her head gravely. "The truth I tell, Child," she said. "The Mistress of Dunscaith ye shall be, for certain." She paused. "But the bowl does not tell if the title springs from his love for you and yer secret deeds together or if ye somehow displace his wife and Lady."

Her heart beat in her throat. She threw her arms around Rhoswen, kissing her tenderly on the cheek. "It matters not," she said. "If I am with him again, they can call me what they will. A title I need not."

Grabbing her shift, she dashed excitedly out of the hut. Through the door, left wide behind her, she heard Rhoswen's final warning. "Let yer heart guide ye, Mistress, but hear also the whispering voice of reason. I fear for ye, Lassie, that I do."

***

The minstrel arrived in the village the very next day, leading an old lean workhorse weighted with the bard's instruments and supplies on its tired back.

He was tall, dark and exceptionally handsome. Gwen and her sister Aillyn recently returned from their work in the fields when they first saw him.

"God in heaven sent us a bountiful gift," Aillyn whispered to Gwen with a giggle, as they both admired his lean build and the large bulge in the front of his pants.

Gwen was surprised to feel the wetness of desire moisten the love-starved triangle of femininity between her legs. A year since she last bedded Rhys and she lain with no man since.

If I must lie with a man to save Rhys, she thought, *this one will do quite well*. She glanced briefly at her golden-haired sister, who gaped with unconcealed lust at the approaching bard.

Gwen quickly pulled Aillyn aside and whispered urgently in her ear. "We should bed this lad together, you and I," she suggested.

Aillyn looked at her sister questioningly. "Mean ye one after the other, or both of us at once?" Gwen noticed a flush of ruddy excitement on her sister's cheeks and a lusty sparkle of adventure in her deep brown eyes.

"Both at once," she replied with a husky laugh. "There is a purpose to this endeavor and you must play your part, dear sister."

"How so, Gwen?" Aillyn inquired with enthusiastic curiosity.

"My future has been told me by old woman Rhoswen," she explained. "I am to bear this minstrel's child which will cause my breasts to swell with milk."

Aillyn looked confused. "I understand not, Sister," she whispered. "Why must we lie together with this man? And, pray tell, why is the milk from yer ample bosom a concern to ye so?"

She looked at Gwen as if she was daft and Gwen laughed lightly.

"It does sound strange, I know," Gwen explained, "but I must be the first to take his seed inside me, when it is most potent. With ye by my side to help with my dire need, my success is all but certain."

Aillyn opened her mouth to speak, but Gwen lifted her hand to shush her, indicating she not yet finished.

"Ye will willingly rear my son, Aillyn - at least for a time," she continued. "If this be true, I beg you share in the baby's conception by lying with his father alongside me."

Aillyn nodded, apparently understanding the logic in what her sister proposed. "But yer milk," she questioned. "Why is yer breast milk of such importance?"

"Because I will need it to nurse the Thane's baby," she replied.

Aillyn looked stunned. "Rhys?" she asked, still confused by her sister's explanation.

"Yes, Aillyn," Gwen replied with confidence. "I will be a nursemaid at Dunscaith and in this fashion I will be reunited finally with my darling Rhys."

***

The bard finished telling his tales and singing his ballads and the crowd which gathered in the village square slowly dispersed. It was a warm summer night and the stars shone in bright competition with the full and majestic rising moon.

The minstrel loaded his packhorse when the two beautiful sisters approached him, with one seductive purpose on both of their lustful minds. As they neared closer, he just fastened the final binding onto the satchel bag that teetered precariously on the straining back of his worn and weary beast.

"Go ye now, Gypsy?" Aillyn asked, stroking the horse's muzzle suggestively while she looked at the handsome gypsy and batted her eyes.

He pulled the leather strap tight, testing its tension and ensuring his load safely secured. He looked thoughtfully at Aillyn before replying.

"Aye, Lassie," he said, his voice deep and confident. His gaze moved from the younger sister to Gwen, who opportunely decided to adjust the front of her low-cut bodice at that very moment. She giggled with feigned embarrassment, pretending the brief exposure of her hard pink nipples inadvertent rather than intentional.

He swallowed hard. "There were none willing to offer a traveling stranger shelter for the night." He shrugged, looking up at the clear night sky. "No matter, ladies, 'tis a clear and mild night." He smiled warmly, patting the flank of his horse affectionately. "Braeden is good company," he laughed. "We will find a tree to rest under together, between this village and the next."

Gwen looked over at Aillyn, who nodded her agreement to whatever her sister was about to propose.

"Minstrel," Gwen cooed sweetly. "My sister and I know a secluded clearing not far from here, where ye might safely rest for the night. If ye wish to follow, we will lead."

As if on cue and without waiting for his response, the two sisters began their walk up the steep hillside toward the dense woods adjacent to the roadside meadow. Looking back over her shoulder, Gwen smiled when she saw the bard and his horse eagerly followed, not too far behind.

***

They led him into the deep forest, following the hint of a path Gwen knew well. She often retreated to the privacy of her woodland sanctuary if she wanted some time alone. The clearing was secluded and difficult to find, which meant she and her sister could thoroughly enjoy the handsome minstrel without fear of discovery or interruption.

"Ladies," he called out, "Ne'er will I find my way back, even in the light of day. I pray there is nothing afoul in your intent!"

They reached the grassy hideaway. Gwen turned to face the traveler, shaking her dark curls loose as she removed the sash securing her hair at the nape of her neck. Pausing briefly for dramatic effect, she unlaced the front of her bodice and unfastened the cotton hooks attaching her skirt to her chemise. With the breathless dignity of a noiseless sigh, her frock glided off her hips and slid silently down her long sexy legs to fall onto the grassy ground around her feet. Since her open bodice no longer served its intended purpose as a covering, she slipped it over her shoulders to let it tumble off her arms and accompany her skirt on the soft forest floor. She stood naked before him now in the glimmering moonlight, her heart pulsated with excitement. She was surprised to feel a trembling wave of exhilaration pass through her, as she realized she yearned to feel his hard cock between her aching legs.

This coupling is a means to an end, she reminded herself. Yet, her body screamed for the sexual release denied her since Rhys left. With shock and delight, she noticed the wet moisture of her desire already trickled down the inside of her thigh. She closed her eyes, cupping her round and voluptuous breasts in her hands, just as Rhys did so many times before when they had been lovers. She circled her nipples with her fingertips, creating a wave of pleasure beginning in her bosom and ended in her pussy. Her entire body tingled with anticipation.

When she opened her eyes, she saw Aillyn, who stripped off her clothing as well, began undressing the minstrel. She laughed to herself. Her sister, only nine months younger than she, shared so many of Gwen's attributes and qualities - good and bad. Physically uninhibited, she enjoyed several lovers although only nineteen. Gwen, playing her role as Aillyn's confidante and tutor, counseled her lusty sibling carefully about the need for discretion and caution in the execution of Aillyn's sexual exploits. Together, they visited old woman Rhoswen often to procure effective potions and extracts to prevent pregnancy, the same remedies Gwen employed when her frequent intimacy with Rhys almost a daily joy.

Aillyn demonstrated her experience with the masculine organ, using the minstrel's cock as the main tool in her educational presentation. After undressing him, she pushed him onto his back on the grass of the clearing with a husky laugh. She was on her knees next to him with his large cock in her mouth, her moans of happiness muffled by the bulky penis filling her hungry orifice. Her long golden hair, which splayed onto his lean torso like the delicate sweeping tentacles of a sea anemone, soaked in the bright moonlight like a thirsty sponge. Saturated, her moon-touched locks radiated a blended combination of chartreuse and yellow that glowed with an otherworldly iridescence. She grasped the thick base of his rigid shaft with one hand, while the fingers of her other urgently stimulated her own rapidly stiffening nipples. As Gwen watched her sister use her sensuous lips and tongue to expertly pleasure the gypsy's hefty masculinity, Gwen's pussy, slick with her wet desire, burned with the aching tingle of hot anticipation.

She could no longer stand aside as an observer. With panting swiftness, she joined her sister on the forest floor. Facing backwards, she straddled the minstrel's face, spreading her drenched labia with the fingers of both hands to expose her rigid and engorged clit. She lowered her pussy onto his waiting lips, moaning with pleasure as she felt his tongue on her stimulated button of pleasure.

Her slick cunt screamed for more. She rocked her pelvis back and forth, sliding her swollen pussy against the rough stubble of his gorgeous face. Her dangling breasts touched lightly on his stomach, tantalized by the titillating contact of his skin on her sensitive nipples. Her face, only inches away from her sister's talented performance on the minstrel's cock, gave her an up-close and unobstructed view of the exciting and inspiring show.

As Gwen took in the full visual impact of her sister's oral talents, she redoubled her efforts on the bard's face. She gripped her sister's hands wrapped around the base of the traveler's rigid joystick for leverage, as she enthusiastically smeared her wet and swollen pussy on his virile jaw. Her climax rapidly built. With a shudder of excitement, she felt the warm tension building rapidly in her burning loins. Then, with startling abruptness, the explosion of pleasure in her pelvis ricocheted with devastating intensity through her entire body. With surprise, she felt an extraordinary gush of release soak the gypsy's mouth and face.

Without realizing, she cried out. Her sister disengaged her lips from the minstrel's cock with a smile.

"You have had your pleasure, then, Sister!" Aillyn laughed. "My turn on his face, please. His cock is yours now to do with as you please!" She winked.

"Aye," Gwen panted, acknowledging her need to have his cock inside her as soon as possible. Without further prompting, she and her sister repositioned themselves at either end of the stunned and overjoyed subject of their sexual attentions.

Aillyn wasted no time. As she smeared her dripping cunt onto the traveler's face, already soaked with the gush of Gwen's copious cum, her moans gave testimony to her own quickly approaching release. Gwen, who hoped for a second orgasm, positioned her twitching pussy on the bard's swollen cockhead. In one smooth movement, she sank herself onto his lengthy pole with a gasp of exhilaration.

Both sisters, in unison, feverishly pursued their mutual ecstasy. Aillyn ground her pussy on the gypsy's face and momentarily Gwen noticed the quivering premonition of her sister's impending release begin in her engorged labia. With a scream, Aillyn pushed her pussy onto the bard's face as her body started to shake. "God in heaven," she cried, as every muscle in her sexy body became preoccupied with the spasm of her heavenly release.

Gwen moved the minstrel's cock in and out of her tight cunt with renewed vigor. "Plant your seed in me now, Bard," she demanded, as she rode his penis like a possessed demon.

He was very obedient. She barely uttered her command, when she felt the warm splash of his cum fill her sexual canal. Pushing his still pulsing penis into the mouth of her cervix, she gasped as she felt the injection of his potent liquid into her fertile womb. The delicious feeling of his cock deep inside her now brought her to the summit. With dizzying satisfaction, she began her fall into the ecstasy of a second release.

"I'm coming now, my darling Rhys!" she shouted, her eyes filled with tears of joy and her cunt consumed with the jism of her salvation.

Her pussy contracted uncontrollably, gripping the minstrel's cock with forceful thankfulness. Her body, wracked with spasms and covered with a thin film of healthy perspiration, glimmered, and glistened in the moonlight.

She laughed to herself. In the throes of passion, she called out his name. *How beautiful and perfect*, she thought to herself. Although she just fucked another man, in her mind he had been Rhys in disguise.

"You have never left me, dear one," she whispered to herself. She withdrew the minstrel's cock, collapsing happily on the soft grass of her wooded sanctuary, right next to her spent and smiling sister.

***

She fell asleep on the chair in the sitting room, waiting for Rhys to emerge from Mahrea's chamber. She awoke with a jolt to find he stood next to her, with Niamh clutched tightly to his chest. He looked visibly shaken, his face white, his lips trembling.

She quickly rose to her feet. "Rhys, what is it?" she asked him with alarm, searching his eyes closely for clues. She glanced downward, her eyes drawn immediately to a bloody gash extending across the knuckles of his left hand.

"Rhys, your hand!" she cried.

He waved away her concern with a smile, taking her hand sadly. "I failed, sweet lady," he answered. "I fear this baby, after all, will be motherless."

Gwen squeezed his left hand with gentle determination. Niamh, still asleep in the secure protection of her father's arms, stirred slightly.

"No, Rhys," she said with firm resolve. "A mother she shall have, may God be my witness!"

She tenderly took the child from Rhys, kissing her lovingly on the cheek.

He looked at her, tears streamed down his cheek. "I am so very pleased you returned, lover." He gazed down, realizing he spoke presumptuously.

She took his face in her hands, fixing her eyes on his. "Yes, Lover," she replied with emphasis. "You have always and will always be my one and only."

And with that final confirmation of their undying love and passion for each other, she took her precious package and retired to the nursery quarters.

Chapter Four
Orb

As he entered his wife's bedchamber with Niamh clasped in his arms, Gwen's words of encouragement faded behind him and echoed in his head. *I love you, Rhys,* her sweet voice said. *My heart is your captive, and your servant it shall always be.* Could their love be rekindled, even as he struggled with the complications of this cursed arranged marriage and the tragedy of a heartbreaking miscarriage? Despite the seemingly insurmountable barriers, he felt a glimmer of hope in his desperate and demoralized heart.

The room was quiet and dark. Since it took his eyes a moment to adjust to the lack of brightness, he deliberately wasted time before closing the heavy wooden door behind him. *Concentrate on your task at hand,* he reminded himself as he braced himself for a difficult confrontation with his callous and obstinate spouse.

The dim light from the sitting room leeched through the open door, a silt-filtered sunbeam barely penetrating the dense and agitated murkiness of a deep ocean. He waited a moment. Now satisfied he could navigate safely without the additional illumination from the firelight of the adjacent chamber, he reached behind him to pull the door shut.

The sound of the door latch, clicked loudly as it made contact with the doorframe, startled him. He imagined himself a prisoner who entered a locked cell. There could be no escape now, until his mission accomplished.

The flames burned down to pulsing orange embers - the weak and sickly remnant of a vigorous and healthy fire now in its final moments of life. He saw the shape of an unlit candle resting on the mantle. Stepping over to the fireplace, he picked up that candle and lit the wick by touching it to an ember. The oily candle-stem flamed eagerly, casting a bright sphere of illumination around Rhys and the child, who rested quietly in his arms.

Squinting, he saw the shadowy silhouette of Mahrea on the bed. Surprised to see she was awake. Instead, she sat cross-legged, her head bowed in intense concentration as she stared intently into a glowing object she held delicately in her cupped hands.

He peered curiously at the peculiar scene. From across the room, his vantage point not ideal, but it seemed to Rhys, Mahrea cradled an egg shaped orb in her lap. The object made of a crystal-like material, he concluded, since he saw the subtle orange flicker of the smoldering cinders reflected in its smooth and glassy surface. It emanated a soft grey light, which surrounded Mahrea like a shielding aura.

In a flash, he was jolted with the shock of recognition. *The object she held in her hands is the same instrument that Caedmon described!* he realized. He recalled Caedmon's description of the scene he witnessed in Iceland, shared striking similarities to the sight Rhys presently beheld. The orb seemed to emit a raw mental energy which completely saturated Mahrea's conscious mind. In fact, she looked as if she willingly succumbed to an all-consuming hypnotic spell.

She was completely naked. *She is beautiful*, Rhys mused, but the attractiveness of her physical form unfortunately diminished by the potency of her belligerent and he feared malevolent soul. *What a shame*, Rhys reflected. From a distance, he admired her glorious nudity, a privilege denied him these past nine months. Sadly, the last time they had lain together was the night they conceived the beautiful baby he held now in his arms.

Her fiery red hair spilled wildly onto her shoulders and breasts, touching her smooth skin like a myriad of groping fingers. The deep and wide maroon circle of silky flesh encircled her tightly hardened nipples matched the color of the red strands brushed over the surface of her generous bosom. She held the object close to her body; in fact, Rhys noticed the smooth glass surface pressed tightly against her nude and exposed femininity. As he watched, she uncrossed her legs - opening them slightly to a frog-legged posture. Her smooth thighs rested flat on her comfortable downy mattress, unwittingly exposing her glistening pussy to his scrutinizing eyes. She rubbed the globe against her wet folds, moaning softly. She seemed to be in some kind of a trance-like state and oblivious to Rhys's presence in the room.

Very odd. As he looked closely at her blatantly uncovered sexuality, he saw no evidence of the traumatic labor she just experienced. Her labia, which should have been swollen and irritated, looked smooth and pink. There was no sign of stretch and tear and no visible blood or staining on her thighs or bedcovers. In fact, her pussy looked unusually virginal. As she pushed the glowing crystal against her luscious cunt, it occurred to Rhys perhaps the object's energy possessed healing powers, repairing whatever damage her vaginal canal sustained during childbirth with unbelievable and unearthly rapidity.

He approached cautiously, unsure of the nature or purpose of the strange globe. *Careful, Rhys*, he cautioned. *God or the devil, more likely, only knows what danger exists in that unnatural radiance!* As he neared closer, he watched Mahrea stare into the glass ball as she gently rubbed it against her sensitive clit. She seemed mesmerized by something she saw inside. He wondered if she was in a trance or simply in shock after her ordeal. *There is unholy and hypnotic magic in the object*, he concluded to himself. He brought the candle closer, shining its light cautiously onto the bed in an attempt to unobtrusively discover the truth.

Mahrea did not acknowledge him. She, either consciously ignoring him or else unaware of his presence due to her preoccupation with the enthralling glass sphere. Rhys quietly laid the candlestick on the bedside table, determined to investigate the mystery further.

He started to reach out with one hand, intending to touch the object and perhaps remove it from Mahrea's grasp. Bracing himself, he rested one knee on the edge of the mattress, clutching Niamh tightly in one arm. As he started towards his goal, he was startled when his fingers touched a solid barrier.

Abruptly, he felt a ripping pain on the back of his hand. He drew his arm away with a jerk, looking at his hand with a combination of confusion and concern. A long gash, which extended along the knuckles of his right hand, throbbed with pain as it started to ooze blood.

Looking up, he did a double take. Instead of empty air, in the exact place where his hand had met the obstruction, Ciara perched like a black sphinx. Somehow, she took up a defensive position between Mahrea and Rhys without being noticed, until now. The dark fur on the back of her neck rose as if brushed with a storm of static and she rested on tense haunches prepared to pounce at a moment's notice.

He studied the cat as his mind struggled to understand what happened. Looking at his hand again, it was apparent the gash made by an animal's claw. Had Mahrea's feline companion materialized out of thin air or had she been there all along? The pitch-black color of her fur easily served as an effective camouflage against a backdrop of darkness and the room was so dimly lit it would have been quite easy for him to mistake her for a shadowy fold in the bedcovers.

Nevertheless, it was odd she appeared so clearly visible now, when a moment before she blended so effectively into her mistress's comforter. *Perhaps the evil beast was conjured by a witch's spell. If so*, he mused, *the sorceress who cast the invocation is sitting right in front of me*. It appeared Mahrea remained in a deep trance. Her eyes transfixed on her magical globe, stayed static.

The people of Skye claimed Mahrea practiced witchcraft and he began to think perhaps they were right. The crystal in her lap was a tool of the dark arts, he felt certain and the black cat nothing less than an enchanter's familiar. *There is danger here and I must be cautious,* he thought to himself. He paused momentarily, as he tried to determine his next move.

***

Even before Mahrea arrived at Dunscaith, rumors circulated she had links to the occult. Granted, the people of Skye were inherently mistrustful and superstitious, had a tendency to view anything unfamiliar with fear and skepticism.

Not only because her veins pumped Viking blood. Her flame-red hair and unusually reserved demeanor were fuel for wild speculation and exaggerated presumptions and Mahrea made no attempts whatsoever to ameliorate the negative impression she made on the local populace. Her foreign heritage and uncommon appearance aside, an odd episode occurred at the remote castle in Iceland when Caedmon traveled with a small diplomatic party to welcome Mahrea as the future Mistress of Skye.

Mahrea's mother, Alfhild, raised her on an icy, but sprawling and comfortable estate on the Icelandic coast. They lived together, the murdered Norwegian King's beautiful mistress and his compelling bastard daughter, in a remote castle on the Nordic island outpost. The mother and child provided every luxury by order of the Norwegian court, wanting for nothing, but in reality, both Mahrea and her mother exiles in a most luxurious prison.

Mahrea's union with Rhys, arranged by Olaf, the Viking Lord of Mann and the Isles, was an arrangement that seemed to benefit all parties involved. Inge Haraldsson, the Norwegian child king, was the only legitimate child of the slain Viking king, Harald Gille. Inge's two half-brothers, being only infants, posed no serious threat to the Norwegian throne for many years. Mahrea, on the other hand, now a woman and as such, she might very well decide to claim her birthright, if given the proper means and the suitable opportunity. Mahrea was an awkward thorn in Norway's side and marrying her to a foreign warlord in a far-off Viking territory in Scotia neutralized a potentially volatile situation. Mahrea's engagement and eventual marriage was a welcome relief to her mother as well. With the threat to Inge, embodied in her beautiful but eccentric daughter removed, Alfhild's banishment from Norway might finally be lifted.

And although Olaf Godredsson certainly strengthened his ties to Norway through the union, the ruthless and unpopular King of Mann and the Isles entertained other motives in mind when he arranged the marriage. By integrating Viking and Gaelic gene pools, Olaf hoped to establish a race of Gall-Gaidheal or "Foreign Gaels" whose blended and unique heritage bound their allegiance to their native land rather than to Norway or Scotland. Olaf, a vassal of the Norwegian king, yearned for autonomy in his rule over the Hebrides and had, in fact, given his own daughter's hand to Somerled - himself a Gael - in order to advance his personal agenda. And Rhys' union with Mahrea, of course, served the same purpose, merging the two cultures in matrimony and perpetuating a new nation of independent "Nordic Gaels" through their anticipated progeny.

Caedmon had not been pleased with the arrangement to say the least. Shaking his head, he warned Rhys a marriage designed by others would end in tragedy for everyone involved.

"My Liege," he said, "your heart belongs to another! Do not do this to yourself, to her, and to the people who love you so dearly. Bow not to another man's whim, my friend."

Rhys shook his head. "There is much you do not know, Caedmon. I have no choice in the matter, for many reasons. I must marry this Viking maiden or else many in this kingdom will suffer the dire consequences. Do not press me on this, my friend."

Caedmon gazed with concern at his friend, furrowing his brow. He laid his hand on Rhys' sleeve, leaning forward in a gesture of secrecy. "There are rumors about the girl, my Liege," he warned. "Although beautiful, they say she has been unable or perhaps unwilling to attract desirable suitors. Despite her fiery beauty, she is aloof and detached. Some say she is a witch!"

"Surely you do not believe such tales, my friend," he replied with nervous laughter. "The girl has been raised in exile and any stories about her have surely been fabricated and exaggerated by her enemies."

"I am simply repeating what I heard, my Liege," Caedmon's voiced his concern. "This match will be ill-fated, I fear."

Rhys' glared at his lieutenant. "I have no choice, Caedmon," he said through clenched teeth and with steely determination. "Morsel is most powerful and his might is reinforced by the crushing strength of Norway's army. If I defy him, we will be overrun and defeated in the blink of an eye. I must agree to this union or else Skye will suffer a most barbaric and bloody fate."

This explanation did not appease Caedmon, who gladly agreed to give his life for his friend and leader in battle, if it came to war. Seeing Caedmon would not let the matter rest, he pulled him aside.

"Caedmon," he said, "Olaf knows about Gwen. He threatened to kill her if I do not agree to this union. I have no choice, my friend."

"Gwen?" Caedmon queried. The concern, evident on his weather-beaten face, reflected his fondness for his general's lover. "He would harm sweet Gwen?" he asked, knowing full well Olaf would not hesitate to carry out this threat.

"You know he would, Caedmon," Rhys replied sadly. "That is why I must marry Mahrea."

"But what have you told her, Rhys?" Caedmon asked, concerned now for Gwen's emotional security.

Rhys almost doubled over with the visceral pang of regret surging through him. He looked down. "I could not bear to tell her in person," he said shamefully. "I sent a messenger with a letter explaining my duty requires this sacrifice of me, but I will love her with my whole heart and soul for the rest of my life."

Caedmon's looked at Rhys with incredulous disbelief. Rhys, with a sinking heart, tried to defend himself. "Caedmon," he argued, "I just couldn't face her. It would have broken my heart to see her reaction to my betrayal. She may have also pressed me on the details," he said, "and I would die first before revealing to her the personal threat prompting this decision."

Caedmon nodded. He seemed to ponder and digest Rhys's logical and heartfelt justification of his actions. "How can I serve you now, my friend?" he asked kindly after a moment of reflection.

"Go to the Nordic outpost, my trusted lieutenant," Rhys said. "Bring gifts to the exiled Princess and welcome her as the new Mistress of Skye. Be wary in your observations, Friend. And when you return," he added, "you will tell me all you surreptitiously gleaned on this your mission."

"I am at your service, my Lord," Caedmon said with a bow. "I will leave first thing in the morning with a small welcoming party."

***

As Rhys stood at his wife's bedside, he recalled Caedmon's recounting of his trip to Iceland and his unsettling observations of Mahrea. Although Caedmon shared the sensitive and shocking portions of the tale with Rhys and Rhys alone, the abridged version of the lieutenant's story became widely publicized after his return to the Isles.

The castle appeared as an icy extension of the frozen coastline. On the day of their arrival, the cold and weary travelers were welcomed into the warm castle interior by Mahrea's mother, Alfhild, who hosted a sumptuous banquet that night, held in their honor. Mahrea, oddly enough, glaringly absent from the festivities. Alfhild, apologized profusely, accepted their gifts graciously and offered excuses and promises for the missing princess. The appeased envoy went to their soft and comfortable beds expecting to meet the exiled Princess in the morning.

Caedmon began to worry when days passed in this fashion. They took meal after meal with their affable hostess and allowed unlimited access to the spacious estate and its frigid grounds. The guests offered every comfort imaginable, wanting for nothing during their brief seven-day stay. But when the end of their visit neared, it appeared Mahrea, for some reason, refused to grant them an audience.

Caedmon was concerned. Was Alfhild keeping her daughter sequestered, for fear something in Mahrea's appearance or character might sabotage the carefully designed marital and political union? Was this inexplicable insistence on privacy a way to ensure their daughter would marry Rhys as planned? Or rather, was the refusal to meet the Gaelic welcoming party Mahrea's own personal preference, due to some kind of anti-social personality flaw?

The night before their departure, Caedmon tossed and turned restlessly in his bed, his troubling thoughts prevented a restful slumber. Finally, he rose in the dead of night, deciding a walk through the deserted halls of the Scandinavian castle might help to clear his mind. He walked slowly, deep in thought as he wondered how to explain their lack of contact with Mahrea to his general when they returned to Dunscaith. *I will be unable to report to him my impressions of a woman I did not even meet!* he thought nervously. Rhys would be sorely disappointed Caedmon failed in his mission.

As he approached the end of the main corridor, he noticed a hazy layer of blue mist swirling around his feet. He realized with alarm he walked through a thin cloud of smoke which, oddly, failed to rise more than six inches from the ground. Frantically searching for the source, he noticed the haze seemed to emanate from a small alcove to the left. Turning the corner, he found himself in a short hallway leading to and ending at an ornate mahogany door. Wisps of the powder blue and odorless smoke drifted from underneath the entryway's threshold and naturally, Caedmon deduced with panicked apprehension a fire must be raging on the other side of the heavy doorway.

Without hesitating, Caedmon pushed open the door and rushed into the room. He searched the chamber quickly with his piercing blue eyes, but found no flames. He stood in a fashionably decorated sitting room, his boots obscured by the same smoky groundcover he encountered in the hallway. It was as if he stood in a shallow pond, his boots submerged in the dark and murky waters of some misty swamp. His mind, struggling to comprehend, concluded the unnatural smoke was not the product of a fire. A soft grey light streamed from the adjacent bedchamber and he decided he must investigate further.

As he approached the door to the bedroom, he heard the sounds of a woman moaning. His curiosity piqued, he crept noiselessly to the door, hiding his body in the corner between the wall and the doorframe. Peering cautiously around the edge of the doorjamb, he realized he procured an unobstructed view into the private bedroom of a beautiful maiden. In an instant, he realized she must be Mahrea.

The Viking princess lay naked on top of her bedcovers, her nude body deliciously exposed in an unconscious display of raw sexuality. Caedmon gasped, withdrawing his gaze from the edge of the door. He hid with his back flush against the wall adjacent to the entryway, his heart pounding with the adrenaline rush surging through his veins. He had not expected to stumble accidentally into such an immodest and private scene and he would have never guessed Mahrea's physical appearance so compelling.

How can it be that such a stunning beauty has no suitors? he wondered. *Perhaps the lure of her extraordinary body cannot overcome some other glaring flaw in her personality*, he reflected. He learned the rumors of her reclusive behavior were not fabricated, given the repetitive absence of the young woman at all of the castle functions for the entire week of the envoy's visit. Was it her awkward reserve keeping the courtiers from pursuing her? Or rather, was it a pathologic and dysfunctional attitude towards conventional socialization norms? *Perhaps this opportunity to be an unnoticed voyeur would somehow clarify the true nature of her eccentricity*, he deduced with excitement.

He was not entirely unaware this line of thinking was in part a poorly concealed justification of the circumstances in which he found himself. It seemed apparent he was now a covert witness to a sexual performance already promised to arouse and titillate. *Caution, Caedmon*, he warned. Although this opportunity to observe the beautiful Mahrea in the throes of her private passion might be viewed with envy by some, he knew he was also in grave danger. If someone discovered his intrusion, he was certain his punishment brutal. *The retribution of my Viking hosts would almost certainly involve torture and death*, the thought chilled him.

He inched himself back to the edge of the doorway, taking every precaution to remain unobserved during this truly inadvertent mission of espionage. He peered into the bedroom again, taking time now to scrutinize the scene with enough attention to detail to allow an accurate and complete report to Rhys upon his return to Skye. He took a moment to carefully examine the peculiar event materializing before his curious and critical visual inspection.

At once, he noticed the smoke, which emanated from an object Mahrea held in her hand, did not rise to the ceiling, as the laws of nature normally commanded. *Despite its lightness of color, it seems to have unnatural density and weight,* he observed with almost scientific curiosity. He watched attentively as it crept like a living entity along the bedcovers, slithering down the side of the bed to finally rest as if exhausted, sprawled with fluid-like diffusion across the floor of the bedroom and stretching lazily into the adjacent room and corridor. A hint of a draft in the room caused the smoky carpet to gently rise and fall with rhythmic monotony, much like the soft and undulating respirations of a sleeping monster.

The finger-like strands of smoke flowing from the round object in her hands caressed her seductive body with a lover's touch. She responded to the contact of the dense smoky projections on her breasts and stomach as if touched by flesh and blood. Moistening her lips with her tongue, she arched her back so her hardened nipples enjoyed the tactile stimulation of the gaseous digits. Caedmon could not believe his eyes. As the dense strands of smoke encircled her ample mounds, he saw the indentation of those uncanny fingers as they contacted her quivering and sensitive breasts. *The smoke is enchanted!* he concluded, as he nervously and eagerly watched the maiden's heated response to its magical touch.

He turned his attention now to the object in her hands, a round crystal which shimmered and gleamed as she pressed it urgently onto her wet pussy. The smoke, which rose evenly from the entire surface of the glassy sphere, seemed to somehow emanate from thousands of embedded and tiny magical pores. The globe also produced a strange and eerie grey illumination, encasing and surrounding Mahrea like the ghostly and supernatural equivalent of a silkworm's cocoon. *Might this object also produce an invisible energy that has resulted in a kind of inebriation?* Caedmon pondered. *Perhaps*, he concluded, since Mahrea seemed entirely oblivious to her surroundings as she moaned and writhed in a trance-like state of sexual preoccupation and ecstasy. She rubbed the sparkling crystal against her visibly stimulated clit, causing to become even more vocal in her fugue-like primal vocalizations.

Caedmon's cock strained against his leggings. Although his mission depending on gathering information, he found himself unable to suppress his natural physical response to the sexual drama unfolding, unbelievably before his very eyes. His eyes widened as he saw Mahrea reach under her pillow. With surprise, he watched her pull out a large candle measuring at least an inch and a half across and eight inches long. He quickly withdrew his head, expecting she light it and in so doing discover his presence in the shadows at her doorstep. However, as the moments passed without any sign of extra illumination from the bedchamber, he cautiously peered around the doorframe again to investigate the situation.

His breath caught in his throat. With one hand, Mahrea stimulated her clit with the smooth glass globe, while with the other, she grasped the base of the candle tightly and inserted it into her soaking wet pussy. Beads of sweat glimmered on her beautifully exposed body, as she gasped with excitement and writhed with pleasure. As she rubbed the obliging crystal against her labia's hooded button of pleasure, she plunged the candle all the way into her soaked cunt. *She is using it as a surrogate cock!* he realized with amazement as he jealously watched her vigorously fuck her engorged and stimulated pussy with the rigid penis-substitute. *She will soon reach her climax!* he concluded, noticing the smooth skin of her tight buttocks tremble with the preface of her impending sexual earthquake. *This beautiful Nordic mistress will come momentarily on her eight-inch shaft of wax!* he accurately predicted as she continued to eagerly plunge the gigantic candle in and out of her dripping vagina.

He couldn't believe he was a witness to such an unrestrained carnal performance. As she worked the crystal avidly against her clit in an astonishing display of erotic self-stimulation, the muscles of her trim thighs began to shake uncontrollably and then, unexpectedly, she removed the wax dildo from her pussy, which started the early metric pulsation of its orgasmic crescendo.

Caedmon gasped with shock and delight. As he watched, Mahrea slid the candle into her posterior orifice. Her tight and quivering anus swallowed all eight inches of the lengthy pleasure stick. As she slid it in and out of her gaping sphincter, the involuntary spasms in her labia intensified with the delicious and involuntary paroxysm of an explosive orgasm.

The forceful stream of her lusty cum saturated her pelvis and buttocks. Her tight anal sphincter gripped the candle forcefully, squeezing the makeshift cock with a series of forceful and rhythmic spasms. "Sweet Hecate," she screamed out in pleasure. *Her body is shaking as if it was actually possessed by the Wiccan goddess!* he commented excitedly to himself, as he watched the conclusion of her breath-taking sexual recital. "Oh fuck," she yelled, as the last gush of her lusty cum made the crystal globe wet and slippery with her glistening moisture.

His heart beating in his throat, Caedmon silently withdrew, fearful the intensity of Mahrea's orgasm broke the trance-like spell and lead to his discovery. He returned to his room, lying awake with his rock hard cock throbbing under the bedclothes. He spent remainder of the night reviewing in his mind the strange performance he witnessed in the Princess's bedroom, which more than once, needless to say, led to his own private release before the sun rose on the eastern horizon.

***

Rhys recalled Caedmon's debriefing on his return to Skye several weeks later. His lieutenant left out none of the details, openly and honestly described the peculiar smoke, the mysterious orb, and, finally, Mahrea's shocking yet exciting dream-like sexual performance.

Rhys, listened carefully, became profoundly concerned about the implications of what he heard. *Could she in fact be engaged somehow in the dark arts?* he remembered thinking. Perhaps she was indeed a witch and the rumors circulating about her true.

None except Caedmon, of course, privy to the disturbing yet arousing scene in Mahrea's bedroom that night, but the entire entourage spoke freely Mahrea's peculiar and insulting reclusiveness. The stories of their cold and icy reception in Iceland were greatly embellished, quickly spawning tales of Mahrea's secretive dabbling in the occult. Thus Mahrea's Wiccan reputation became established, many months prior to her actual arrival at the castle.

Rhys quickly reviewed this information mentally, as he stood by Mahrea's bedside trying to plot his next strategy. He could not take the orb from her, since the vicious feline would undoubtedly thwart a second such attempt. *And after-all, would it be prudent to awake her thus from such a hypnotic trance?* he pondered. *Like a disoriented sleepwalker, she might become violent if awoken abruptly from her fugue-like state.*

I could simply leave, he thought, but knew avoidance solved nothing. *I need to confront Mahrea now*, he concluded. Gripping the baby close to his chest, he cleared his throat before speaking.

"Mahrea," he said loudly. "Awaken now, and greet your husband and baby."

She continued to stare into the orb, oblivious to his calls. He tried again, but there was still no visible effect on her trance-like preoccupation with the crystal globe.

Realizing he must knock the ball out of her hands, he fashioned an idea. Balancing himself on one leg, he took the vigilante Ciara completely off-guard. In a flash, one boot-clad foot landed squarely on the cat's chest, knocking her off balance and pushing her backwards into her mistress's lap. The cat crashed against Mahrea and the orb. The globe forcefully displaced from Mahrea's grasp by the stunned feline, tumbled out of Mahrea's lap and rolled innocently onto the bedcovers next to her.

The spell was instantly broken, at the exact moment Mahrea's attention disengaged from the orb's powerful enchantment. She was nonplussed for no more than a split second. Not at all surprised now to find him standing at her bedside, she glared at him coldly.

She did not speak a word, studying him like a panther assessing her prey. After a moment of awkward silence, he realized he needed to initiate the conversation.

She looked curiously calm, given the traumatic labor she recently endured. *Shock, perhaps?* he pondered, as he examined her unsettling composure. *No*, he concluded. *This is some form of complacent and gratified intoxication, induced by the power of her evil bewitching stone*, he mused.

He decided to give her the benefit of the doubt. *Is that the salty remnant of dried tears softly powdering her pale smooth cheeks?* he wondered sympathetically. Looking closer, he thought again. The dominant emotion etched in her delicate features was anger rather than fear, but nevertheless, he planned to give her a chance to embrace the miracle of her new daughter before he drew any false conclusions.

He cautiously approached her with Niamh safely pressed to his chest, sat on the edge of her bed with tenuous and wary vigilance. He reached towards her tenderly, intending to brush the wet strands of maroon hair from her flushed but stony face.

Her reaction jolted him, physically and emotionally. With lightning speed, she prevented his well-intended contact with vicious and determined interception. She clutched his right hand with aggressive and irate hostility, causing a ripple of pain to shoot from his fresh injury up into his shoulder and neck. He grimaced, but said nothing, being unwilling to give her the pleasure of hearing a verbal outcry.

He tried to pull away, but her hand a vice gripping him with uncanny strength. Her steel-blue eyes, normally cold and detached, transformed to two branding irons threatening to scald and scorch with their piercing and malicious gaze. He felt she looked into his very soul and he shivered with dread. *Ridiculous*, he reassured himself. *You are a powerful and respected warlord, and this woman cannot and will not control you!*

Still, he mustered all of his strength to break her uncanny spell. With a deliberate effort of will, he released his hand from her death-grip and rose defiantly above her at the bedside.

"I am your husband, Woman and your Lord," he boomed. "How dare you defy my efforts to console you!"

"I may be your wife, Thane," she hissed defiantly, "but I will not submit to you as a servant does to her Master. When we wed, you were as aware as I that your equal I would be. The Norwegian king, my half-brother, dictated it should be so!"

"Hold your tongue, Wife," he said. "This talk will get us nowhere. I bring you your daughter, who will suckle at your breast now, may God be my witness."

Her chilling laugh bellowed. Rolling over onto her side, she stifled her uncontrollable cackles in her thick down-filled pillow.

He looked at her silently, shaken to his core, as her laughter gradually subsided. Finally, she raised herself to a sitting position, leaning against the massive wooden headboard, and locking his gaze.

"God has no sway here, my foolish husband," she sneered. "I serve no one, Thane, but myself.

And evil Hecate! he thought, shuddering to hear her blasphemous words. Somehow, despite his fear, distress, and anger, he managed a calm reply. "My Lady," he said evenly, persisting in his hopeful plea to whatever trace of humanity resided within her, "we have a beautiful daughter and for this blessing we must thank our gracious God. We shall name her Niamh and she will be our bright light, Mahrea."

"Take her away," she replied coldly. "I can never love her, knowing she lived and he died."

"Surely you cannot mean this!" he said incredulously. "She is ours, Mahrea and to decline God's precious gift would be blasphemy and a sin against all right and good!"

"Take her to the nursemaids, Husband," she said through clenched teeth, the mounting irritation audible in her callous voice. "It would be ill-advised for you to persist in such an unwise and foolish vein. You know me not, Thane," she warned, "and it would not go well for you to insist on testing me further." As she spoke, the globe pulsed ominously with red and throbbing emphasis.

Ciara, now recovered from the blow she sustained from Rhys' boot, reiterated her mistress' not-so-subtly veiled threat by baring her teeth and hissing menacingly. And then, without warning, she lunged like a heat-seeking missile intent on single-minded destruction. Rhys, reacted to the rapidly approaching threat, staggered backward with surprise. The cat's sharp and talented claws, which almost certainly inflicted potent and potentially deadly injury to Niamh's fragile new-born flesh, thankfully missed their mark, unproductively scratched the thick leather of Rhys' knee-high boots instead.

There is unnatural danger here I cannot fight with my warrior's weapons, he realized, his heart filled with sadness as well as fear. Without another word, he clutched Niamh tightly and retreated to the tenuous and questionable safety of the antechamber.

Chapter Five
Bryon's Beautiful Daughter

His sleep was restless, troubled by his unsuccessful and unsettling confrontation with Mahrea. *Surely, there must be unnatural humors coursing through the veins of a mother who does not feel a bond to her own child!* he thought, unable to comprehend Mahrea's outright rejection of the sweet new-born. Mahrea's blatant demonstration of her heartless and malevolent soul shook him to the core. *What will I do now?* he wondered with apprehension. He was trapped in a loveless marriage with a woman who, not only cold-hearted and merciless, but also wicked and depraved. *God help me!* he silently prayed.

And the orb. How could one explain such an object without invoking the unnatural? Its powers seemed limitless. It pleasured, enthralled, protected, cloaked, illuminated and for all Rhys knew, it might also encompass the power to see the past and predict the future! Mahrea gazed into the depths of the orb's glimmering core as if she observed some kind of a vision reflected in its mysterious nucleus. *Perhaps she can visit the past in the brilliant interior of her glowing crystal,* he thought. The very thought made him shudder with fear. *If so, all is lost!* he concluded with despair as his thoughts turned to his passionate affair with Gwen and the danger to both of them if Mahrea somehow gained knowledge of their past.

Try as he might, he found no rest. His thoughts raced through the events of the day, until they found their exhausted but joyous resting place in the antechamber outside of Mahrea's bedroom. *Sweet Gwen*, he thought happily, how unexpected and welcome it was to see her after so many years! Gwenhwyvar means white, pure, and smooth, like her alabaster skin which he longed to kiss and caress again as her lover and partner. "Gwen, my one true love," he whispered, returned now to raise his new baby and perhaps to give new meaning to his sad tragic life.

Three years passed since the first time he laid eyes on her. *Oh, what I would not give to relive that fine day and that beautiful night!* he thought wistfully. As the first bashful rays of sunlight streamed timidly through his bedroom window, his weary mind drifted off into a deep yet fitful sleep and as he started to dream, his wish granted.

***

Snow: a dense and brilliant white cloud of impenetrable precipitation swirled like a vortex, blinding his vision with frigid and bleaching indiscretion. He closed his eyes as his mind reeled seemingly partnered with the wild dance of snow around him. He winced as an unrelenting barrage of miniature daggers of blowing ice pierced his skin. He shivered, surprisingly and abruptly, dismissed the blizzard of confusion until a moment ago, embraced him like a jealous spouse.

Opening his eyes with tenuous caution, he was relieved to find himself on a horse riding at a leisurely pace through a meadow on a hot and humid summer day. His heart pounded in his chest. He recognized the scene, a vivid and accurate recounting of his first meeting with the beautiful Gwenhwyvar.

His custom was to periodically venture unaccompanied into the countryside, masquerading as a penniless traveler. He wandered to all four corners of his beloved Isle of Skye, conversing with his peasant subjects as a peer rather than their lord. They often confided in him, usually referencing their Thane in a positive light, but sometimes divulging their frustrations and worries to their newfound friend. Rhys always learned much, using the knowledge he gathered to improve his governing skills and enrich the lives of the serfs who served him with such loyalty.

It was early morning and although he spent the night in a lean-to, he felt refreshed and rejuvenated. He steered his horse across the meadow, emerging from the grassy hillock to join a small group of farmers on the main dirt path.

"Hail, friends," he called out to them with a smile. "May I join you as you walk, on this fine but hot August morning?"

Two of the men looked to be in their late forties or early fifties, while the other two were just lads of fifteen or sixteen. *Two Da's and their sons*, he concluded, *probably going to tend to their fields.* Each of the two men held hoes and one of the lads carried a shovel. The other boy, whose muscles attested to his strength, pushed a cart packed high with tensely filled burlap bags. *Wheat for a late planting*, Rhys thought, as he dismounted from his horse to walk alongside the four serfs.

"Aye, you may," said one of the men. He was solid and stocky, with a full head of greying hair and a thick beard to match. He offered his hand to greet Rhys while he smiled broadly. "I am Bryon," he said, "and the lad, Aiden, is my son." He pointed by way of explanation to the boy with the cart. "This is Cael, my brother and his son, Dillan," he said, as he gestured towards the other two. All three of Bryon's companions nodded pleasantly to Rhys as Bryon introduced them and Rhys, in turn, bowed his head slightly in polite acknowledgement.

"I am very pleased to meet you, Bryon," Rhys responded, addressing the good-natured farmer since he seemed to be the leader of the small group. "I am Dugal," he lied, using his usual traveling alias as he gripped Bryon's hand with firm and friendly pressure. "I have traveled alone for many days and I yearn for a bit of company."

"Where go ye?" asked Bryon.

"To the coast," Rhys replied, "to join my brother who is a fisherman. Sadly, I lost all of my possessions, except for this old but trusty nag, in a fire and my brother has kindly offered to take me in."

Bryon nodded, "These are difficult times, Traveler. Our harvest was poor, due to heavy rains in July. We must plant winter wheat, so we can pay the required tithe to the Thane of Skye."

Rhys felt a pang of remorse. *These good people struggle to survive, yet they bravely strive to meet their obligations.* He took in a breath before continuing. "You are worthy and loyal, good farmer," he said. "Perhaps the laird will require less in payments this season, if the harvest was poor."

"Perhaps," Bryon replied. "He is a noble and just thane. Regardless, we have our cross to bear. Ne'er will we shirk our responsibility."

At that moment, there was a sudden commotion on the path ahead of them. They reached the top of a small rise in the hilly terrain and they saw not over to the descending continuation of the path. On the other side, they heard the sound of hoof-beats and the curses of futile pursuers.

Realizing a skittish horse most likely heading their way, the small group scrambled to move aside before the animal galloped over the hill, but without sufficient forewarning, the last minute attempt to avert disaster was only a partial success. Aiden, found it difficult to maneuver the heavy and cumbersome grain-laden cart, hastily abandoned it in his rush to safety and the wheelbarrow, rested in the dead center of the path, represented an unavoidable and dangerous obstacle to the fleeing horse emerging momentarily over the crest of the hill. Meanwhile, Rhys was experiencing his own difficulties. Try as he might, he simply could not persuade his slow-moving mare to evacuate the unhindered dirt roadway for the uninviting tangle of dense brush on the pathway's shoulder.

In a cloud of dusty confusion, the frightened charging beast came careening over the hill's summit. As predicted, the panicked steed galloped headlong into the farm cart which clipped the animal's front legs as he attempted, a moment too late, to leap over the obstruction. The horse, whose airborne trajectory, altered by the unavoidable contact with the wheelbarrow, veered to his left, crashing forcefully into Rhys' nag. Like perfectly positioned dominoes, the horse toppled Rhys' nag and she, in turn, crashed directly onto Rhys like a two-ton stone. Rhys knocked backward and the last thing he remembered was a searing pain at the back of his head, as he soon succumbed to the black amnesia of unconsciousness.

***

When he awoke, his head throbbed. As he opened his eyes, the blurry outline of a face swam in his field of vision like an indistinct reflection on the rippling surface of a pond. He strained to focus and in a moment he recognized the friendly and concerned face which looked down upon him.

"Bryon," Rhys said with some difficulty. His mouth dry and his head throbbed.

The farmer offered him a cup containing cool water which Rhys accepted gratefully, draining the contents with noisy and thankful gulps. Bryon quickly refilled the cup from a large jug at his side, offered it to Rhys with a look of concern in his kind brown eyes. Rhys nodded his thanks as he drank the second serving leisurely, less hurried now his thirst partially satisfied.

Rhys realized he lay recumbent on a bed of hay, inside a small and modest barn. Covered thoughtfully with a blanket, his neck, which pained him to move even a fraction of an inch, supported with a burlap bag stuffed with feathers. With some difficulty, he propped himself partially upright on his elbows with a quiet moan. A tacky, adherent spider web fog of disorientation muddled his brain and entrapped his mind's awareness. Like the stray feathers taken up their stubborn residence in his hair, it took some time to brush away the confusion.

He looked around in an attempt at orientation. "I have been moved," he said groggily, concluding the obvious.

Bryon smiled. "You have indeed been moved, Dugal," he confirmed with amusement.

"What happened to me on the pathway, Friend?" Rhys asked, having no recollection whatsoever of the events following his concussion.

"Fortunately, Traveler, you were thrown backwards by yer horse's momentum," Bryon explained.

"Thrown backwards?" he questioned, finding it difficult to remember the events.

"Yes," Bryon confirmed. "Your horse stumbled forcefully against you before losing her balance, thankfully throwing you clear of her falling body with the unintentional push." He paused, looking at Rhys with a furrowed brow. "Both beasts broke their hind legs and their injuries could'na be repaired." He looked down sadly. "Aye, there was na' we could do for the poor brutes." His voice trailed off, the implication obvious.

Rhys processed this information. "She was a loyal beast," he commented with sadness. "I shall miss her sorely."

"You can'na' complete your journey on foot," Bryon pondered. "I have will lend you my mule and my son. I pray you will accept my offer."

The farmer's kindness touched Rhys. "Aye," he agreed, smiling warmly. "I give you my word they will both be returned to you safely." Rhys smiled to himself, knowing full well he planned repay the peasant's kindness with half a dozen horses as well as forgiveness of the next three season's tithes.

"You must rest a day before you go," Bryon said. "You took a hard knock, Friend!"

Rhys rubbed the back of his aching head, feeling the large and painful knot forming where his skull joined his neck. He knew some sleep would speed the healing.

"Thank you, Bryon," he said. "I will rest now and leave at the break of dawn."

"Good," said the farmer. "'Tis midday now. I will send for you to sup with us at our evening meal."

Bryon rose to take his leave and Rhys, exhausted, fell fast asleep as soon as his eyelids closed.

***

He awoke to the sound of someone calling and after a moment of confusion, he realized Bryon said his name. *Dugal*, he chucked silently, the name he had chosen so long ago for his peasant alter ego. He shook off the haze of sleep, realizing as he did so his head no longer ached. Opening his eyes, he saw Bryon at the barn door.

"Dugal," he called. "Be ye strong enough to join us for supper?"

"Aye, friend," Rhys replied. He got up slowly, surprised to feel the room spin as soon as he stood upright. Bryon was at his side in an instant, stabilizing him from behind with an arm around his chest. The sensation of dizziness passed quickly.

"I am fine now," Rhys said quietly. "If you lead, I will follow."

Bryon released his grip, staying by his side to prevent a fall for the first few steps. Rhys, feeling stronger, walked with sturdy determination towards the barn door.

Bryon laughed. "You are strong and stubborn, I'll give you that!"

They walked together down a small grassy path leading to a modest cottage with a thatched roof evenly layered with meticulous care. Soft wisps of smoke drifted from the chimney into the darkening summer sky - evidence of the cooking fire now burning low. The smell of mealtime filled the air and the aroma of the evening meal reminded Rhys he had not eaten for a day and a half. His hunger gripped him with its needy hands, pleading now for attention like an irritable child. As Bryon pushed open the cottage door, the promise of nourishment swept from the room to welcome them like a gracious maître de.

The large room crowded with the strain of accommodating a family of five. A sturdy wooden table, with a bench on either side, formed the centerpiece and on it sat a steaming roasted chicken on a large platter, a loaf of bread, a pitcher of ale, and an enormous bowl heaped with steaming vegetables. Rhys glanced around the room, noticing a fireplace situated immediately adjacent to the table, boasting a generous hearth open on both sides. A large cot in the corner to the right, obviously belonging to Bryon and his wife, with three smaller cots positioned one next to the other in parallel, lined up against the opposite wall to the left.

Bryon's wife stood on the far side of the table, her ruddy face beamed a smiling welcome. On either side of her stood Bryon's son, Aiden and an attractive girl with blonde hair who was probably sixteen or seventeen years old. Another girl with dark walnut hair bent over the fireplace, her back turned as she cooled the smoldering coals with water from a clay jug. Her task completed, the dark-haired girl stood, wiping her hands efficiently on her apron. Turning, she took her place next to her sister to greet the injured traveler.

Rhys felt a figurative kick in the gut. Although he sustained no blow, he struggled with his breath and his head reeled with the dizzying impact of her dangerous, devastating beauty. The room spun around him, he feared he would pass out momentarily. His heart pounded against his constricted chest, causing his face to flush with the surge of blood flowing into his giddy brain. He heard Bryon's voice, but his words distant and muted seemingly transmitted through the distortion of thick molasses.

"Dugal!" Bryon called. "You look peaked. Sit ye down, Lad."

He felt Bryon's arm on his, easing him down onto the bench on the near side of the table. His mouth dry, but the dizziness passed. Bryon's wife poured him a mug of ale, which he drank thankfully as he tried to collect his thoughts and control the powerful emotion threatening to overwhelm and consume.

He glanced with amazement at Bryon's beautiful daughter. Her inviting rich and lush eyes saturated with a color not unlike the deep blue of a purple iris. Her gaze locked his, which caused his heart to leap into his throat. This single glance from this dark and sultry beauty transformed his dreary palette from a crude ink sketch into a colorful oil-on-canvas masterpiece. Her violet eyes, whose deeply penetrating look, painted a rich and vibrant pastel masterwork on the canvas of his yearning soul in the brief span of a single second.

She brushed some dark strands of walnut hair from her forehead as she parted her full maroon lips to flash him a bright and friendly smile. Her teeth were as white as a dogwood blossom and her skin was the creamy shade of a vanilla rose. Her cotton shift, designed for comfort in hot weather, did little to conceal her enticing curves. Her cheeks flush red as his eyes moved from her face to her visible and generous cleavage. Not meaning to embarrass her, he quickly disengaged his glance as he hastily turned his attention back to Bryon.

"My apologies, Bryon," he stammered. "I am still feeling feint I fear, despite my comfortable rest in your barn all this long day," he said. "I am better now, thanks to your ale and your kind hospitality."

Bryon clapped him on the back. "Some food should help, Laddie," the farmer said. "Bonnie cooked our finest chicken to give you strength."

Rhys nodded his thanks to Bryon's wife. "You are too kind, Lady," Rhys said with a smile. "I must admit to a strong hunger!"

Bryon laughed. "Sit down, one and all," he ordered, "and we will sup with our newfound friend." He sat to Byron's left and Bonnie's right. Bryon's three children sat on the opposite bench and the stunning brunette, to Rhys's delight, sat directly across from him.

"My eldest, Gwenhwyvar," Bryon said as he pointed to the dark-haired beauty. "We call her Gwen, for short."

Gwen nodded shyly, although Rhys thought he noticed a twinkle of excitement in her eyes as she met his stare for a third time.

"Aillyn is our middle child," Bryon explained, "and you have already met my son, Aiden." The two other children smiled as their father introduced them.

"I am truly pleased to meet you all," Rhys replied politely. "I am forever indebted to you, for your hospitality and kindness."

"Eat, friend," Bryon replied, "and then you will rest again. My home is yours."

Bonnie deftly brandished the cutlery like a warrior demonstrating her awesome proficiency with deadly weaponry. When all the plates piled high with chicken, bread, and vegetables, Bryon uttered a short prayer. Afterwards, they all ate silently, intent on the blessing of nourishment set before them.

Rhys continued to gaze at the beautiful Gwen as they ate. As discreetly as possible, he studied her warm violet eyes, her alluring and prominent cheekbones, the sensuous fullness of her pouting lips, the way the delicate muscles of her neck tapered into her delightfully exposed collarbones and generous heaving bosom. He flushed with unexpected emotion, as her eye caught his for one overwhelming and fleeting second. *What is it about this beautiful woman that has moved me so?* he asked, unfamiliar with the overpowering passion her simple look elicited in his thumping and love-struck heart. He felt dizzy again, as the impact of her presence so close rolled over his entire being like a crashing ocean wave threatening to drown him with the proximity of her sensuality.

When her glance met his, he felt an unexplainable connection to her, almost as if they knew each other for many long years. He was drawn to her, like iron to a magnet and she was a force he simply unable to resist. He wondered how he could arrange to speak with her alone, if only for a brief moment. Perhaps if he shared his feeling of deja vu with her, she would reciprocate with some insight to explain the pull she created in his lovesick heart.

They finished eating and he would return shortly to his bed of hay to rest before his long journey home in the morning. Rising to thank his host and hostess, Rhys looked intently into those violet eyes as he spoke.

"My thanks, family," he said. "Perhaps we will have the chance to meet again and share much more than a simple meal together." He looked at Gwen as he finished his mug of ale, hoping she deciphered his message. Her response to his unspoken proposition was a barely perceptible smile, which to Rhys seemed subtly seductive. *I think she shares my feelings*, he thought hopefully. Perhaps she would somehow find a way for them to meet privately, although he feared this hope simply a far-fetched fantasy concocted by his hopelessly romantic soul.

Bryon led him back to the barn, his lantern lighting the short winding path to his makeshift sleeping quarters. Exhausted, Rhys returned to sleep as soon as his head touched the feather-filled burlap pillow.

***

He awoke with a start, feeling a warm and moist pressure on his lips and a firm wet probing in his mouth. He hastened to recover from his initial disorientation, realizing he engaged in a very real and passionate kiss not occurring in a dream or a fantasy.

Opening his eyes, he found himself under a shimmering umbrella of walnut hair. *Gwen!* he realized with grateful happiness. He held her face in his hands as he reciprocated her tenderness with the searching exploration of his own tongue in her mouth. She moaned with satisfaction, pressing her lips against his with urgent excitement.

She pulled her face away, allowing him to see her kneel beside him. With initial shock, he realized her nudeness. She removed her thin cotton dress, discarded it on the hay next to her. The moonlight shone through a solitary window high in the rafters of the barn, casting enough light onto her glorious nakedness for Rhys to admire her incredible and unmatched beauty. Amazed by what he observed, he felt joyous tears moisten his eyes and gently trickle down his cheeks. "You are my one and only," he confessed quietly, surprising himself with words formed on his lips, somehow, with automatic and natural ease. *You are meant for each other, now and for all eternity!* His deepest soul informed him quietly and in a moment, they would consummate their everlasting and perpetual love affair.

Her hands found his tunic and without saying a word she pulled it over his head, baring his lean but muscular chest. She grasped at his trousers as well and in a moment, she removed them, pulling them off his legs and discarding them along with his tunic, next to her dress on the hay.

Now naked, his cock aroused to a full rigid ten-inch erection and once again, she surprised him with her boldness. Before he had time to react, he felt her lips encircle his thick and throbbing organ. He felt his cock push against the soft and accommodating cradle of her tonsils as she took the entire length of his virile manhood into her mouth and down her throat. He moaned with appreciation as she squeezed his aching balls with her fingers and rubbed the tip of his cock with the silky wetness of her pharynx. Her pursed lips gripped his penis like a closed fist, giving him an oral hand-job he would never forget. She started at the base, slowly sliding his cock out of her orifice, only to reinsert his large organ by gliding her lips from his bulbous cockhead back to the base again. She repeated this process again and again, only more quickly with each cycle. *I am fucking her mouth with my rigid ten-inch organ!* he gasped with excitement as he felt his orgasm build. *I want to come, but not yet!* he warned. He gently held her head in his hands, extracting his aching tool from her accommodating mouth. "I need to feel my cock in your pussy!" he panted.

He pulled her body on top of his, kissing her lips with hot and burning desire. She pushed her hard nipples against his strong chest, a maneuver that seemed to arouse her passion to new heights. He felt a gush of wetness soak his pubis as she pushed her dripping pussy against his pelvic bone. Gripping his cock with both hands, she answered his plea with reciprocal urgency. "I agree," she said with breathy urgency. "I want your manhood deep inside my throbbing cunt!"

Rhys embraced her, rolling them over as one entity so he was now positioned on top of her. She splayed her legs open while encircling them around his hips, as he pressed his cock against her pleading sexual entrance.

"Fuck me hard and deep," she implored. "I wanted you from the moment our gazes met. I am yours, sweet lover, now and forever!"

"I am your servant, Lady," he said, "and I will gladly do your bidding. You and I are meant for each other and I will show you my love by giving you the pleasure of a powerful release."

She wept. "I have waited for you, all these long years!" she said. "Put your cock inside me now... I cannot wait any longer!"

His rigid cock rested in the silky groove of her pleading labia - much like a diver, whose perfect linear form poised and ready for his pointed and speedy descent from the cliff-edge into a wet, deep ocean destination. He slid his sexual instrument along the slick canyon of her burning slit, preparing for the moment of penetration into her love-soaked feminine ravine. She moved beneath him, thrusting her pelvis upward as she helped him stimulate her dripping lips with his gliding bulky cockhead. As he pushed his manhood against her engorged clit, she writhed with excitement as she anticipated the deeper fulfillment of his ten-inch cock in her willing and waiting cunt.

She grasped his buttocks with both hands, urgently encouraging his penile incursion into her quivering chasm. He could not deny her. Abruptly, he plunged his hard and aching cock into the wet tightness of her burning pussy. She gasped as he pushed himself completely into her sexual canal, submerging all ten inches of his talented weapon to the hilt. Feeling her body tremble against him, he worried his bulky organ might be causing her pain.

"My sweet Gwen," he whispered gently into her ear, "why are you trembling so?"

"Your cock touched my deepest soul," she replied. "I need you now! Fuck me, Dugal," she begged, "and make me come!"

"I am Rhys," he confessed. "I have been sent to you from heaven to satisfy your body as well as your soul."

He felt her eyes search for his in the incomplete darkness. "Why have you two names, mysterious stranger?" she asked. "Are there secrets you hide that should make me fear you?"

"No danger here, sweet maiden," he replied, "only love and tenderness!"

She kissed him deeply, taking his head in her hand. "I know you not, but I trust you completely," she said, her lips still pressed lightly on his. "I feel as if we have known each other for centuries."

"My feelings are the same," he replied. "I have much to tell you, Maiden, but the time is not yet ripe for explanations."

She seemed to accept these words. "Rhys," she said, as if testing how the word sounded when spoken. "Rhys is a fine name, Traveler," she concluded, "and one which you share with our kind Thane."

He laughed, kissed her again as he pushed his cock deeper, feeling the rounded receptacle of her cervix warmly embrace his engorged and burning cockhead. He would reveal his identity shortly, but not until then, they both enjoyed their mutual ecstasy.

He moved his penis in and out of her slippery and lubricated pussy with delicious repetition. He withdrew his engorged stiffness completely and after a split second pause, he sank his lengthy instrument of pleasure back into her soft and accommodating pelvis. Each thrust elicited a small cry of pleasure from the sexy recipient of his rhythmic and talented attentions.

"Harder," she begged. "Make me come, sweet lover!"

He redoubled his efforts. She bucked wildly underneath him like a filly in heat being serviced by her favorite stallion. His muscular torso rippled with sweaty exertion. He raised himself over her, holding her wrists above her head on their bed of hay as he passionately kissed her ruby lips and explored her panting mouth with his tongue. Her breasts were like twin mountain peaks, which jutted from the sweat soaked plateau of her rib cage with glorious magnificence. He rested his pounding chest on her rock hard nipples, gliding his wet, tense skin over her aroused and stimulated protrusions. Looking in her eyes, he recognized the excitement building within her. He did not need her verbal confirmation to realize her orgasm coming momentarily.

"Oh, Rhys," she exclaimed. "Don't stop, I'm coming now!"

Her vagina squeezed tightly around his thrusting cock. Heeding her instructions, he kept pumping as he felt her release explode around his forceful labor. Her fountainous stream of cum gushed out of her orifice with surprising intensity. In an instant, his balls soaked with her luscious secretions. She started to scream, but he suppressed her vocal outcry with a stifling kiss, concerned the exuberant sounds of her ecstasy would awaken the entire village.

Her body wracked with quivering contractions as her vagina continued to pump his cock, like an ambitious and over-exuberant milkmaid attempting to squeeze the milk from a resistant bovine teat. The stimulation of her gripping vagina would shortly produce the intended result - a squirting and streaming reward - the envy of any lusty milkmaid.

Rhys's balls contracted, as his steaming cum ejected into his rigid loading chamber. His revolver cocked, the bullets ready and the trigger pulled. A delicious burning tightness gripped his entire manhood, followed by a body-shattering and uncontrollable release. His cum propelled with vigorous force and surprising power, gushed against the back of her sexual canal and into the small opening of her sensitive cervix. She gasped with astonishment, as his penis impelled wildly to discharge his remaining voluminous ejaculate with rapid-fire weaponry.

"I feel your cum," she cried with surprise, "and it is so incredibly sexy!" Her body trembled now. "My sweet God in heaven, feeling your wetness inside me is making me come again!"

She wrapped her legs tightly around him as her body contracted with a series of involuntary spasms. Rhys, who was still coming, buried his face in Gwen's generous bosom as he felt a surge of emotion discharge through his entire body. He felt his love for her fill his soul and being and overwhelmed, he sobbed uncontrollably onto her warm soft shoulder.

"Oh, my sweet dream lover," she cried, caressing his wet cheeks with tenderness. "You fill me so completely. Today is the happiest day of my life and I will never forget you!"

Spent, they lay side by side, his exhausted penis still inserted in her quivering and satiated vagina, hard yet, but rapidly returning to its pre-erection softness. He never felt so alive and complete. He held her tight, as the contented promise of post-coital sleep began to seduce his tired and satisfied body.

She rested in his arms, but for a few moments only. "I must go," she finally said. "My family may wake and their questions will be difficult to answer."

He nodded his understanding. "In the morning then, my love, I will dream of you."

She already slipped her dress over her head. "And I of you, my darling Rhys!" She left as quickly as she arrived. *She changed my life forever*, he thought as he drifted into a deep and restful slumber.

***

The morning sky was clear and the air less humid. The mule, loaded with supplies for the two-day journey, grunted its annoyance at being awoken at such an early hour. Rhys, feeling refreshed after his night's adventure, enjoyed a light breakfast with Bryon and his family. Gwen, who sat across from him again at the kitchen table, gave an impressively nonchalant performance given the intimacy they shared just hours before. Her conspiratorial glances infused with hot passion and loving tenderness went unnoticed by the rest of the family as they busied themselves with the morning meal. Her looks in his direction made his cock hard and heart ache. *Oh how I love and desire her!* He must find a way to see her again, he knew... and soon.

They shared a moment alone as Aiden loaded the mule for the two-day journey to Dunscaith. "I will send you a message," he said to her quietly, "which will be delivered along with a gift for your father."

She nodded her understanding. As he and Aiden guided the mule down a gentle embankment to the main road, Rhys felt the pull of her beautiful spirit touch his deepest soul. Looking back, he saw she cried.

Very soon, maiden, he whispered. *We will be together soon!*

Chapter Six
A Welcome Intruder

Rhys continued to dream, but rather than a vivid and accurate narrative of his past experiences, his dreaming became a surrealistic decoupage of images and memories. The six horses he gifted to Bryon galloped in perfect formation, tail to muzzle in a unified linear entity instantaneously transformed into a fire-breathing serpent. The transmutation sprouted a set of gigantic leathery wings which the monster flapped in furious frustration. Although the rushing wind from the beating wings raised a blinding cloud of purple dust, the frantic beast could not lift itself off the ground.

Turning its head to look behind, the dragon recognized the impediment to becoming airborne. Slung over its back was a heavy hemp cord carried on either end a weighty burden on the one side, hung three massive bags overflowing with gold coins. Rhys observed the scene his sleeping mind constructed, knew immediately the bags represented the three years of tithe forgiveness he granted Bryon, as thanks for his hospitality that hot August night. On the other side of the rope, Rhys recognized the letter he sent along with the gifts for Bryon - addressed in his own hand to his sweet Gwen. The note weighed close to nothing and seemed to somehow act as an unlikely but effective counterweight to the hefty bags of gold dangling on the other side of the serpent's body.

The dragon bared its jagged and glimmering teeth. Each tooth, a shining knife-blade in miniature, gleamed with blinding brightness in the sunlight. With a violent twist of its neck, the beast reached backwards to clench the rope firmly in its lethal jaws and with a snap, the rope abruptly severed in two, allowing the bags to drop with a crash onto the dusty roadway.

The coins spilled onto the path, somehow multiplying as they hit the dirt highway such that the brown road became suddenly paved in gold. The letter drifted silently onto the golden surface, as the dragon lifted itself into the air with one decisive flap of its massive and liberated wings.

The letter quivered, as if alive and overcome with overwhelming emotion. Rhys, now an active participant in his dream, stood over the note and with some hesitation, bent over to pick it up. Before his fingers reached the fluttering paper, the note unfolded itself and became a large puddle of clear water. Rhys, on his hands and knees, peered into the puddle with curious amazement. He saw people and objects in the shimmering liquid, but the images were blurred and distorted, as if he viewed them through eyes fogged with the curse of severely near-sighted vision.

He peered more intently, after rubbing his eyes with closed fists. Suddenly, the images came into sharp focus almost as if the puddle were a camera lens finally adjusted by its photographer to the correct distance setting and f-stop. His heart beat with excitement as he recognized Gwen's beautiful profile in close-up. Her eyes scanned something as if she read a note or a message. Tears moistened her deep blue eyes, but she smiled and her face seemed flushed with excitement.

My letter! Rhys thought with joyful recollection. *She is reading the letter I sent with the gifts to her father!* In it, he professed his undying love for her, promising to send Caedmon within a fortnight to bring her secretly to Dunscaith for their first clandestine rendezvous. In the message, he also, of course, revealed his true identity, asking her to keep this secret between them, at least for a time.

He longed for her so, he recalled, surprised to feel the heartache of separation in his dream-infused imaginings reliving this emotion from his past. He laughed to himself. He had not been able to wait a fortnight, dispatching Caedmon the very next day to retrieve his lover from her distant cottage in the countryside. Although he met her just a few short days earlier, it seemed like an eternity. Their first reunion, a passionate and joyous affair, marked the beginning of a long and intense love affair and from that time forward, they never separated for more than one week at a time.

He studied her beautiful face depicted in the mystical puddle. The joy radiated from her visage. It literally shone in discreetly visible and oddly palpable sunbeams, warming his face and gratefully soaking into his thirsty skin. He closed his eyes, basking in her positive energy like a lizard lying on a sun-baked stone. In his slumbering mind, he likened himself to a chameleon whose skin changed from a cold and stony grey to a vibrant and warm green, in response to her transforming aura. He embraced her joyous emotion, allowing it to renovate the tired and dreary house of his weary soul. Her infectious elation inoculated itself into the core of his being, causing him to weep with joy. His teardrops dripped gratefully onto the reflecting pool and rippled the surface with exaggerated intensity.

With panic, he saw her image in the puddle became blurred by the wavy interference of his tears which fell like raindrops from a torrential downpour. *You must control this emotional outburst*, his id scolded. *The puddle has more to show, so dry your tears, Warlord!* Heeding his inner voice, he closed his eyelids against the drenching wetness spouted from his tear-ducts. He willed his emotions into a quiet corner of his heart and opened his eyes with tentative anticipation.

His tears stopped and he found himself gazing into Gwen's deep lavender eyes. *No*, he screamed silently, *it cannot be!* Her expression suddenly changed and her own eyes moist with tears. She read another letter, but the tears she now shed born of sorrow, not of joy.

The uncanny intuition of his subconscious told him immediately she held his letter of regret in her hands. The pain on her face was literally visible. In horror, he watched as deep ruts of heartache etched into her smooth cheeks. Horrifying markings made on a perfect block of malleable artist's clay by an untrained and inexperienced sculptor. As he gazed upon the disfiguring ruts the invisible fingers carved into her beautiful face, her skin transformed from clay into a mask of dripping wax. The artist's bony fingers - no longer invisible - smoothed the waxy cheeks, repairing the damage with the mystical talent of a single touch. Then, in one smooth motion, the fingers peeled the mask of wax from his lover's face.

With shock and dismay, he stared at Mahrea's face rather than Gwen's image in the reflecting pool! His wife wore a spiteful smile and her cruel grey eyes danced with mocking laughter. Bent on his knees over the pool, Rhys jumped to his feet, startled by such an unexpected and unpleasant substitute vision. Turning away, he hoped to avoid a confrontation, but alas, the dream's script could not be altered.

Mahrea emerged from her watery prison with the sole purpose, blocking his intended escape path. Although the air was still, her wild red hair blew across her face and her flowing black gown flapped noisily against its own heavy fabric, as if agitated by the wind from a raging storm. She held out her arm, hand raised and fingers pointed towards him in a gesture that literally froze him in his tracks. *I cannot move!* he realized in horror. Try as he might, his legs, stiff and sluggish, simply refused to respond to his desperate mental commands. *Run!* he screamed silently. *You must flee now, before she shows you more!* But her potent and indissoluble spell rendered him her helpless and impotent prisoner.

He realized she spoke, but at first he did not hear her words, perhaps because the glimmering orb she held in her other hand, distracted him. She lifted the globe slowly and deliberately, raising it carefully as a precious religious relic. The crystal rocked hypnotically back and forth, causing him to focus exclusively on its gleaming surface. In its depths, he saw Mahrea's lips move as they recited words continuing to fall on his curiously deaf ears. Letters and words swirled around her busy mouth. *My letter*, he realized suddenly. *She is reading my own words, but I cannot hear!*

Abruptly, her words audible, but the voice was not hers. As her lips mouthed the words, he heard his own voice reading the letter of regret he sent to Gwen, ending their joyous romance. The words rang in his head, uttered in his voice but spitefully punctuated by the mocking and contemptuous expression on Mahrea's face. He covered his ears, but this action seemed to intensify rather than abrogate the noisy and disturbing soliloquy echoing in his brain.

My darling Gwen, he heard Mahrea proclaim in his own voice.

His eyes closed, but this tactic did little to silence the searing pain of his words throbbing like the relentless torture of a migraine headache.

My heart is filled with sadness. You truly touched my body and my soul with the gentle and loving fingers of your pure and beautiful spirit. You have been and will always be my one and only.

I have been given a task and I cannot refuse. I must bend to his order or else suffer the dire consequences. The good people of Skye must live in peace. This is their right. My duty to them supersedes my own happiness, if fear.

I am betrothed, my darling lover, to the illegitimate daughter of our Viking king. I like it not, but I cannot change my unfortunate destiny. We shall be wed this summer and she will sadly come to Dunscaith as my wife and the new Mistress of Skye.

We must end our happy romance, my dear sweet Gwen. I know we must never meet again and my heart breaks with sorrow to think I will never again gaze into the depths of your lavender eyes. Forget me not, dearest lady. Even when you find your happiness with another man, think of me sometimes and recall my pure and true passion for you.

Your love resides in my heart and there it will stay until the day I die.

Rhys.

The globe rocked violently now in her hands; clearly, she was no longer in control. The mistress now the servant, her tool became the master. Realizing her defeat, she released the orb, which hovered in the air unsupported, defiantly autonomous and poised for some evil purpose.

Mahrea gazed at her open palms, smoking with the singeing heat from the fiery crystal she just released. She inspected her hands with detached curiosity. The flesh was raw and bleeding, but the fresh burns caused her no pain. And, although her inappropriately nonchalant laugh sent chills of fear down his spine, the globe seemed to represent a much more imminent threat than his twisted spouse.

The spinning crystal, aflame like a burning miniature dwarf star, advanced towards him with ominous intent. He felt the intense heat on his face and with it a strange concomitant barrage of scolding retribution. The heat relentlessly scalded his skin and burned deeply to reach into his very soul, quickly replaced by his own inner voice, chiding him for his unforgivable past. His regrets burned hotter than the crackling orb and his guilt seared with more intensity than the makeshift sun radiating a mere inch from his sweat-soaked face.

His body crumpled in defeat on the dusty ground. Covering his head with his arms in a panicked reflex, he discovered the shell of his limbs provided no protection whatsoever against the emotional and cerebral offensive that battered his vulnerable and susceptible psyche. The regret and guilt surged through his body with a lethal current. He wept bitterly, praying for forgiveness and for the relentless assault to cease.

How could I betray her love? he sobbed, as the remorse hammered his beaten body with the pounding force of a thousand sledge-hammers. But the betrayal delved deeper, he realized. He forfeited the rich fortune of his own happiness in exchange for the cheap and vacuous pittance of political expediency. He sold out their destiny and their future together, just as Judas in the garden of Gethsemane. He was filled with self-loathing and remorse, horrified by the monster within him who so callously discarded the only true and pure entity in his life.

His heart throbbed with the pain of regret, self-contempt, guilt, and yearning. Oh how he wished he could undo the past. His pleading conscience begged him for redemption. *I must right these wrongs!* he told himself tearfully.

It is not too late, Thane! his persistent ego whispered in reply. *She returned in order to fulfill your mutual destiny together!*

His heart pounded with relief and excitement. Lifting his head, he opened his eyes, confirmed with relief the globe and Mahrea were gone.

Night descended. The clear sky blinked with the cool reassurance of thousands of innumerable stars and a gentle breeze cooled his burning skin.

It is not too late! he repeated. Smiling, he rose to his feet and wiped the sweat from his forehead with a sigh of relief.

All was quiet. Feeling exhausted, he noticed with grateful surprise his bed waited for him at the side of the road, sheets turned down and pillows fluffed. His clothes somehow stripped from his body and he found himself naked in the deserted landscape, a solitary figure in the vast loneliness of his slumbering imagination.

The soft breeze cooled his feverish skin, touching his exposed nudity with the stimulating intimacy of a lover's fingers. Looking down at his naked genitals, he noticed his cock fully aroused. His exhaustion, however, trumped his sexuality and after stroking his penis three or four times his straining physical need temporized as he relented to the comforting and downy seduction of his waiting bed.

And in his dream, he fell fast asleep.

***

He awoke with a start, the reason uncertain. His cock painfully rigid, but surely he had not been jolted to wakefulness by this routine nightly phenomenon. Had his door been opened and then closed, perhaps? This explanation seemed quite plausible. If the creak of the heavy door swinging awkwardly on stiff and complaining iron hinges had not woken him, the noisy click of the turning door handle would have easily succeeded in this task instead.

He quietly reached for his dagger, remaining where he stashed it underneath his pillow. Gripping the hilt with hasty but silent determination, he carefully removed the covers from his lean and muscular nudity, swinging his legs over the edge of the bed to rest his feet solidly on the carpeted stone floor. The darkness of the room meant he slept the entire day. He crouched next to his bed, listening intently for any sound indicating the presence of a concealed enemy.

The fire burned down, but it still cast a dim semicircle of illumination onto the space in front of the massive hearth. He peered carefully into the blackness, his heart pounding as the adrenaline surged through his soldier's veins. Rhys had enemies, but could they realistically penetrate the flesh and stone barriers securing his might castle fortress? *Unlikely*, he mused. But if they had, they might easily find the unguarded sleeping Thane and cut his throat as he slumbered. *I must begin posting a guard outside my chambers,* he thought. He resolved to meet with Caedmon come sunrise and make some long overdue and necessary changes to the castle's glaringly lax security.

He saw a shadow cast vaguely upon the carpeted sitting area in front of the fireplace. He grasped his dagger firmly, raised it to a defensive position in front of him as he stood to face his assassin. "Who goes there?" he called out. "Show thyself, intruder and face your Thane and warlord in hand to hand combat."

The shadow's owner stepped boldly into the dying light of the fire. Rhys dropped his dagger. His heartbeat quickened, but not from fear. *Sweet Gwen,* his soul cried out, a most welcome and sorely missed intruder standing before him in her glorious and seductive nakedness.

"Gwen," he stammered, temporarily rendered speechless by the astonishing appearance of this unexpected but long-awaited visitor to his bedchamber. His recollection of her beauty, although vivid, paled in comparison with the stunning nude reality before his hungry and love-starved eyes. She smiled, offering herself to him with natural comfort and innocence combined with the promise of uninhibited and wanton passion.

"Are you sure?" he whispered, his voice thick with emotion and eager with hope. "What of your husband, Gwen..." he started, his sentence trailing off with dismay as he braced himself for news of her binding intimacy with another man.

She laughed. "I have no husband, Rhys!" She paused, taking two steps toward him in the dim flickering firelight.

"But your son..." he said, slow to comprehend the meaning of her seemingly incomprehensible statement.

"My child was fathered in the usual fashion..." she explained vaguely, "but, alas, he is being raised fatherless."

He struggled to understand this riddle. "Dead, then?" he asked. *Perhaps he was killed by some unfortunate accident or at the hand of an enemy's sword,* he reasoned, postulating quietly to himself.

Directly in front of him, she shook her head in answer to his question as she took his hands in hers, squeezing gently. *She is trembling*, he realized. Suddenly, he knew she borne her child out of wedlock.

"Dear sweet Gwen," he whispered. "I care not about your past!" he said reassuringly. "No shame, my one and only," he said in her ear. "Please, tell me all."

Her face buried in his shoulder and her warm and moist tears traveled on his strong and comforting neck. He stroked her hair tenderly, urging her with his non-judgmental affection to bare her heart and soul.

She gave her confession in the hushed sanctity of his loving embrace. "You are my husband, Rhys," she said, "in every sense of the word. In my heart, we have been wed since the moment I gave myself to you that night in the barn, so long ago."

"Yes," he murmured. "We are ancient lovers, Gwen. There is no one, in this life or any other, who can take your place at my side and in my soul."

Silence. Looking up to meet his gaze, her face flushed with emotion and wet with salty regret.

"I love you, Rhys," she proclaimed.

"And I, you," he confirmed. "There is nothing you can say to me and nothing you have to reveal that would change how I feel about you."

She nodded and taking a breath in, she continued. "He was a passing minstrel. I loved him not and when he caused my shaking release, I called out your name."

"Go on," he urged. "I judge you not, fair maiden. After all, I married, so why should you not enjoy the company of one man or many men, for that matter, if your desire wished it thus?"

She shook her head. "He was the only one, Rhys," she said sadly. "My fortune was told to me by an old soothsayer who instructed I should bed the minstrel to unlock and open the door to my destiny with you."

"How so?" he asked, perplexed again by the puzzle of an incomplete explanation.

She laughed, amused by his understandable confusion. "I know it sounds strange," she admitted, "but the old woman saw my son in her telling bowl, knowing his birth would cause my breasts to fill and overflow with milk," she explained. "She foretold my arrival at Dunscaith as Niamh's nursemaid and knew I would need to bear my own child to make the spring of nourishment for your beautiful daughter flow like fountains from my voluptuous teats."

She pushed her nipples against his naked muscular chest, pulling him against her with her palpable and pressing need.

He held her tight, allowing the inebriating feel of her skin touching on his to completely permeate his vulnerable and romance-deprived senses. *Such intoxication!* he thought, wanting more than anything to drink in her sexuality with reckless and excessive abandon, as he had done so many times before in years long past.

"Oh how I have missed you, Gwen!" he sobbed. He cried now, recalling in a rush the oppressive feelings of guilt, remorse, and regret he just experienced in his dream. "I am so sorry," he apologized with heartfelt sadness. "I betrayed our love, tossing it aside for empty obligations inconsequential in comparison."

She stroked his cheek with her forgiving hand. "It matters not, my darling," she cooed tenderly. "We are together now and you are forgiven, many times over!"

Her lips touched on his and she pressed his aroused and rigid cock against her moist femininity. She drew him down onto the carpeted stone floor, directly in front of the fire's persistent but fading warmth, resting herself on her back while she bent her knees and pulled up her legs with both hands. Suddenly, she spread her legs wide, splaying her limbs apart like a shepherdess eagerly opening her fleecing shears. Her own woolly coat trimmed close, as if the sympathetic example of her clipped and shaven labia might corral the wild and bleating beast of his straining erection.

Her fervid yearning flesh sang for his sweet and searching tongue, much like the resonant and pining intonations of a lonely mermaid whose mortal lover lost at sea. Her drenched pussy moaned with desire, calling with insistence for the return of his storm-tossed ship. Her primal sexuality was a lighthouse beacon and he a floundering boat soon finding safe haven in the harbor of her alluring pelvis.

His face between her legs, he took a moment to savor and admire the awe-inspiring sight. The tender lips of her closely shaved labia like the gentle and delicate folds of a tropical orchid, awaiting the restorative sunshine of his talented tongue. Like the Sun God Ra, the vigorous and stimulating rays of his oral decree soon awakening her slumbering petals, causing her vulnerable blossoms to swell with grateful arousal. Crouching at the apex of her femininity, he offered his prayer at her altar of desire. Encircling his arms around her thighs, he grasped her hips with both hands in order to push her pelvis against his eager face. The intoxicating floral perfume wafted from the luscious flower of her pussy and her taste, heavenly nectar meant only for a God. His head spun with the dizzying emotion of this familiar and sorely missed contact with the silky flesh of her flower-like receptacle. He paused briefly to enjoy the deliciousness of the moment.

The time arrived to embark on the delightful task at hand. He deftly plied the petals of her labia apart with the tip of his searching tongue, luxuriously lapping the wetness of her excitement like a honeybee exploring the hidden richness of an orchid's floral juices with his searching proboscis. He felt the arousal in her parted folds, now engorged and tense with the rushing, heated inflow of her eager circulation. He probed the hooded recess at the pinnacle of her slit until he triumphantly uncovered her still diminutive, but rapidly growing stamen of pleasure. She moaned with delight, assisting his efforts by exposing the pistil of her clit with the helpful traction of her fingers. She pulled her parted lips upwards, which pushed the discreet erection of her stimulated filament and anther forward out of its cradle-like and silky corolla, directly into his worker-bee mouth.

He grasped her sensitive clit with his teeth, flicked and licked it with his tongue until she trembled with excitement. The flesh of her pussy, drenched with her sweet and delicious desire, quivered with the early precursor of a magnificent and powerful release. She pushed her dripping labia against his lips, grinding her pelvis against him with uninhibited and heated enthusiasm. Despite her shallow and rapid breathing, she urged him on with her vocal commands.

"Make me come, Rhys," she moaned, "as you have done so many times before. How I have missed your tongue on my clit! Please, Lover, touch me inside while you eat my cunt," she pleaded. "I want your fingers in my pussy and in my ass."

She spread her legs wide, releasing her fingers from her vertex as she raised her parted limbs into the air. Her busy hands pulled apart her smooth and shapely buttock cheeks to expose the puckered entrance to her tight virgin anus. Her request for anal stimulation surprised him. Although their sexual intimacy always exciting and uninhibited, she never asked him for posterior penetration.

His heart pounded in his chest. While his tongue and lips continued to stimulate her throbbing clitoris, he moved the fingers of both hands into position. Her pussy twitched with anticipation and the streaming moisture from her aching crevice lubricated her anal orifice as well. He inserted two fingers from his right hand into her soaking vagina, while he simultaneously slid the third finger from his left into her tight alternative canal. She gasped with delight when she felt the welcome intruder, inviting deeper penetration into her unexplored territory by spreading her cheeks widely and pushing her buttocks onto his exploring digit. His left finger submerged in her anal canal up to the knuckle as the two fingers of his other hand busy in her tightening cunt. He found the sensitive ridge of roughness on the anterior surface of her vagina, which he rubbed and caressed with talented persistence.

He sensed her orgasm would be strong and intense, judging from the extraordinary grip he felt around his fingers from her contracting vagina and anus. He redoubled his efforts, stimulating her g-spot with the tips of his fingers while his flicking tongue successfully brought her clitoris into a state of glorious full arousal. He moved his finger in and out of her lubricated anal canal, causing her to pant with the mounting expectation of an imminent release.

"Fuck my ass with your finger, Rhys," she cried. "Oh God in heaven, you're making me come!"

He felt the strong contractions of both cavities squeeze tightly around his fingers. A thousand tiny muscles trembled in her groin, buttocks, and vulva, as he felt a warm gush of her ecstasy soak his face and chest. Her body wracked with spasms and she screamed with pleasure. The stream of her cum squirted like a fountain into his mouth, still engaged between her bucking legs. She cried out again, as the gripping pressure on his fingers started to relax.

"Oh my God, I'm still coming!" she exclaimed as she pulled him up, hungrily licking her lusty secretions from the rough stubble of his face. She shuddered, sighing with satisfaction as her intensely fulfilling release came to its gratifying conclusion.

She turned herself over, raising her shapely ass in a primal invitation he was quick to answer. His painfully aroused cock found its home without delay in her wet and throbbing pussy. He fucked her hard as she matched his thrusts with equal exuberance.

"Fuck me, Lover," she screamed. "Ram your hard cock in my pussy and my ass!" she cried. "I want your cum to explode in my ass!"

He couldn't believe what he heard. *Her passion and lust are unmatched. I must have her for my own somehow, for all of my remaining days!*

He felt the tension building in his balls, indicating his release fast approaching. Complying with her eager request, he quickly withdrew his penis from her damp cunt, placing it with determination on her quivering sphincter. Using firm pressure, he slid his penis slowly into her willing posterior entrance. She was well-lubricated and a brief moment later his cock submerged to its hilt in her tight and sexy orifice.

"Oh Rhys, your bulk fills me completely!" she cried. "Fuck me now and your thrusting cock in my ass will give me a second release!"

His cock moved in and out of her ass and the feeling exquisite. Her tightening grip on his thrusting manhood put him over the edge and there was no return. He felt his testicles squeeze the semen into his penis, accompanied by a wonderfully painful tightening in his loins. A split second later, the spasms of his stimulated masculinity pumped a voluminous amount of jism into her sexy canal, providing additional lubrication for Gwen's journey towards a second orgasm.

She panted again as she pushed her buttocks forcefully against him to meet the rhythm of his repetitive penetration. He reached underneath her, finding the engorged button of her rigid clit with his fingers. He rubbed her labial nipple with his hand and continued to fuck her anus with renewed energy.

Her body tensed and her clit palpably aroused. "Don't stop!" she moaned. "I am coming again!"

He felt another gush of moisture soak his hand and spray onto his balls. Her body wracked with another set of spasms. "I love you Rhys," she cried out as her hips quivered uncontrollably. "You are my only lover, potent warlord!" she exclaimed. "You are my master and I am yours to do with as you please, now and forever!"

"No, sweet maiden," he replied. "I am your servant and you are my mistress," he replied. "This truth has been written in the stars, and will never change."

He extracted his shuddering organ from her quivering canal, turning her towards him to lie face to face on the carpet in front of the fire. He kissed her tenderly, stroked her hair, and caressed her face in their moment of post-coital ecstasy.

"But Mahrea," she said, with a worried look. "What about Mahrea?"

What would he do about Mahrea? he wondered. This was a difficult question, and for the moment there was no easy answer.

No matter, he thought. *God's will shall be done and the right path will show itself when the time is right.*

He kissed her passionately. "Worry not, Gwen," he reassured her. "All will end as it should."

As they fell asleep in each other's arms, he wondered if it really would.

Chapter Seven
Sorceress

The confrontation with Rhys had been nothing more than an annoyance and an inconvenience. Without giving him a second thought, Mahrea took to her bed, resting without interruption for the entire day. Her sleep was deep and dreamless. She awoke at nightfall feeling refreshed and invigorated, ready to ponder her next strategy given the unexpected and irritating turn of events.

She stood naked in front of a roaring fire her maidservant expertly stoked. The white flames cast a warm heat onto her youthful body, but did little to melt the iciness of her heartless core. Motionless like a marble statue, her alabaster curves chiseled with precision and perfectly reflecting her chilling and stony heart.

She laughed to herself. *Enough heat.* She much preferred the cold, even more now since her forced exit from her frozen Scandinavian home for this intolerably temperate climate. *And all because of him*, she thought with contempt.

Her disdain was not for Rhys in particular. Her scorn directed at the universe and by definition Rhys included. It mattered little he was noble, honest, kind, and compassionate. Rhys' appealing disposition and purity of his spirit were irrelevant factors, since her distorted and noxious viewpoint colored by her egotistical and vindictive soul. She never desired a mate, but agreed to the arranged marriage only because the union was approved by her coven. Her Wiccan brethren, anxious to extend their base of power beyond the confines of their icy island, happily encouraged her marriage to the Gaelic warlord. After her final initiation, marking her passage from novice and student to mistress and teacher, her crystal forged using the transmuted power of her own psychic and sexual energy. The globe amplified and focused her telepathic and supernatural talents. It functioned primarily as a mental appendage that housed and augmented her unearthly abilities. Her orb saw into the past, predicted the future, protected, healed, excited, and stimulated, cursed, injured, killed, and of course, focused and consolidated. It was a fully integrated component of her arcane power and energy; without it, her mystical strength would be reduced greatly by many orders of magnitude.

Such potent and awesome power concentrated in a single ball of glass! she pondered enthusiastically. She padded with quiet smugness in her bare feet to the corner of her bedroom, stopping for a moment to admire her beautiful body in the full length reflecting glass hanging on the wall. Her pregnancy and the subsequent trauma of delivering twins left no sign on her flawless body, thanks to the healing power of her magical sphere. Her stomach no longer protuberant, but flat and toned, her vagina and labia, which earlier in the morning been stretched and swollen, returned to virgin-like tone and tautness - the painful rip the first child's exiting caused between her vagina and anus miraculously and instantaneously healed. *All this*, she laughed, *due to the simple touch of cold and potent glass on my injured flesh and skin!*

She ran her fingers lightly over her nipples quickly making them hard and rigid. She moved her palms lovingly to the undersurface of both voluptuous breasts, admiring the feel of their weighty fullness as they rested in the cup of her fondling hands. She smoothed a path over the ridge of her ribcage, moved her hands into the valley-like depression of her navel then lower yet, ending at the seductive triangle of seduction where her slim thighs met the inviting shadow of her sexy pubis. She closed her eyes, moaned as she touched herself and moistened her ruby lips with the wetness of her agile tongue.

I have no use for a man, she reflected with cold conceit, smugly satisfied she did not need to require another's touch to bring her the satisfaction she easily gave herself in private. She routinely pleasured herself, by using her fingers, the orb, and various sundry objects - the combination invariably brought her to an intense and fulfilling solitary release. By using items mimicking the size and length of a bulky penis, she always gave herself a thorough fuck without the need for the annoying and inane interpersonal interaction the man connected to a flesh and blood cock demanded. And, of course, her precious globe intensified and enhanced her inward focus, which greatly magnified her self-induced ecstasy.

Although she normally refrained from shared sexual intimacy, one notable and memorable exception to this preference haunted her memory. She paused for a moment in front of the mirror to fondly reflect on her induction ceremony.

Her training as a sorceress took place secretly, over the course of several arduous years of training, beginning at the age of eighteen. Servants conscripted willingly into service from the surrounding desolate countryside tended to her and her mother, both of them exiled to the frozen reaches of Iceland, but pampered with all the luxuries and comforts of royalty. Her handmaiden, Siv, was a quiet young woman, perhaps ten years older than the young princess. Tall and fair, she tended to Mahrea's every need, silent, reserved to an extreme, hesitant when questioned, and almost impossible to engage in conversation. She performed her tasks with precision and efficiency, amenable to any request voiced by her young mistress. Mahrea became very fond of her servant and with time they began to share their confidences with each other in private, beginning when Mahrea reached sexual maturity to become a strikingly beautiful young woman.

Siv taught Mahrea how to pleasure herself, instructing her in the art of self-fulfillment by demonstrating exactly where to touch in order to achieve maximum stimulation and what to insert into her virgin pussy and anus in order to induce the strongest variety of orgasm. Siv's naked body became an example for Mahrea's sexual experimentation. They practiced on with each other nightly until Mahrea became exceedingly proficient at inducing her own orgasms, as well as Siv's. During one of their mutual pleasuring sessions, Siv spoke to her pupil about the coven.

"Young mistress," she began, "your talents are hidden to most, but obvious and transparent to my discerning eye."

Mahrea cocked her head, curious and intrigued by this cryptic comment from her friend, servant, tutor, and lover. "I understand not, Siv," she said, "unless you refer to the physical pleasures we share. Indeed, our private touches take place in secret, but are well-known to you, the sole recipient!"

Siv shook her head. "I speak of talents which extend beyond the physical, Mahrea."

"How so, Teacher?" the girl inquired.

"There is awesome power in your touch and in your eyes," she stated. "A powerful enchantress lies dormant within you and calls to be awakened!"

Mahrea felt a surge of excitement rush through her veins. "An enchantress?" she asked. "What must I do?"

"You must do what I did," Siv replied. "The training is difficult and must take place in secret. The masters of our coven will eagerly instruct you, but you must give of yourself completely to uncloak the richness of your hidden gifts."

Without hesitation, Mahrea replied. "I am willing, Siv. I will offer my body and soul to this greater purpose."

Siv was her sponsor, leading her by the hand through the darkness of the secret tunnels under the castle every night, her blazing energy orb glowing brightly in her outstretched palm to light their winding path. Mahrea yearned to encompass a similar crystal partner which she knew she must earn by succeeding in the tasks and trials she would soon face. Each night, Siv escorted her through the confusing maze of passageways, finally to the hidden caverns, deep under the frozen mountainside.

She took her tutelage to the central cave; the entire coven partook in her wicked education. They gave freely of their diabolical knowledge and soon, she learned the supernatural and the physical inextricably linked. She quickly realized one could not unlock the power of the psyche without the concurrent liberation of one's primal sexuality. The notorious Princess Mahrea, an eager and darkly gifted student, rapidly became versed and proficient in the practice and execution of the black arts.

Night after night, she took her education in the torch-lit cavern, naked in front of her silent robed audience as she demonstrated her speedily maturing skills. She expertly cast complex skills, invoked terrifying curses, and channeled her dark and nebulous spiritual energy forward and backward in time. She proudly flaunted her seductive nudity, as a means to focus and concentrate her paranormal abilities. Lying on a pallet in the center of the Wiccan circle, she laid supine with her legs spread wide apart and her pubis fully exposed, stimulating herself in public whilst her psychic energies churned. As her excitement reached the apex, it culminated in the thrill of a gushing orgasm deliciously witnessed by all, her sexual climax accompanied by a surge of otherworldly clairvoyance and energy exuded from her very core. With each orgasm, her mental powers intensified and her sorcery skills matured until she finally reached the point of readiness for her final initiation.

"It is time for your final task," Siv told her one night. "The masters determined you are prepared. Tonight, dear sister, you will make your own crystal power globe."

Mahrea inhaled. She worked hard and her efforts finally bore the sweet fruit of her labors. "I am ready," she proclaimed. "Tell me what I must do!"

Siv smiled, a wicked lust in her eyes. "You will take your place in the center of our circle, naked, and exposed for all to see."

Mahrea licked her lips seductively with her tongue, knowing full well there must be more. "This I have done, Siv, each night for these many long months. Tell me now, Sister, what will be expected of me."

Siv laughed lasciviously. "You will lie with the three great masters on the pallet and they will help you create your orb."

"Help me?" Mahrea asked, craving more details.

"Yes," Siv replied. "They will fuck you, all three at once, in full view of our gathered crowd. And as they bring you to your shattering climax, they will merge their donated energies with yours to make a most powerful crystal."

Mahrea nodded; her heart beat with excitement. "I am ready now, Siv. Lead me to my three cocks, so I might feed on the salty pumping nourishment of a triple ejaculation!"

Siv snickered. "You are hungry, just as I was, for the feel of their manhood in your mouth and deep inside you."

"Yes, I am indeed hungry for cock, but also for the long-awaited consolidation of my supernatural power," Mahrea replied. "Take me now, Siv, to my final test!"

Her friend led her down the winding passageway into the familiar coven's den for her lusty initiation.

***

She stood on the pallet, her pussy already moist with the wetness of her eager anticipation. The three great master warlocks gathered around her, one on each side and one behind. They were naked and all three wore faces that were not their own. Through some form of enchantment, they fabricated masks which produced a remarkable and realistic transformation. The sorcerer to her right donned the icy white beard and flowing hair of Odin, the legendary Viking magus. The enchanter to her left wore hair the color of red seaweed with a beard matching the color and the texture of ocean kelp. And the wizard behind her, whose rigid cock touching on her enticing and firm heart-shaped buttocks, had two horns growing from his forehead interrupting the wild locks of golden hair framing his chiseled face and jaw.

The fiery haired warlock on Mahrea's left side lifted her in his strong and massive arms with Atlas-like strength raised her high into the air and over his head with effortless ease. She rested on his hands, balanced on her back at a perpendicular angle to his arms, her slender body formed the upper stroke of a *T*, while his toned and muscular bulk created the supporting down-stroke of the same letter. Her nipples tingled and her pussy throbbed as she felt the greedy eyes of the entire gathering inspect her deliciously exposed and lust inspiring physique. He rotated her slightly to the left and then to the right. Her nudity displayed and he presented her to the coven like a sacrificial virgin.

"Behold," Odin boomed. "The gods of old prepare our initiate. We will guide her through the coven's rite of passage!"

There was a murmur of lusty approval from the crowd as he continued. "I am Odin," he proclaimed, "and I traveled long and far to arrive at Mimir's well at the roots of Yggdrasil. I will sample Mimir's liquid and drink the water of her spirit and my brothers will join me." He motioned with an open palm, first to the red-bearded warlock who balanced Mahrea on his powerful arms and then to the blonde who stood slightly behind. "This is Thor the Strong, also known as *Thunderer* and meet Freyr, his cousin - the horned God of fertility!"

A rousing and enthusiastic applause emerged from the gathering. Odin raised his hand, ordering silence. "Watch now, brethren," he commanded, "as we administer our potent liquid. Behold, as we all three bring our initiate, known to us as Mimir, to the heights of her uninhibited ecstasy. And witness, audience, as her physical, mental, and sexual power takes its final form in her crystal orb."

Freyr was on his back, his monstrous twelve-inch cock pointed straight in the air like the fixed and resolute sword Excalibur. His sexual weapon inextricably planted into the stone, firm and solid, stiff and steady - the perfect weapon for the soft and yielding flesh of its feminine target.

Thor handled Mahrea easily. His biceps undulated like the current of an ocean's riptide, as he rotated her over in the air like Neptune twirling his trident. He still grasped her over his head, but his hands supported her as she faced downward, one palm pressed firmly against her heaving bosom while the other cupped between her legs, his fingers on her wet and quivering labia. He lowered her gently, positioning her pooling cunt directly over Freyr's ready shaft. She spread her legs, using her fingers to move her slippery lips aside, opening her slick channel for the welcome penetration of the warrior's spear.

Thor released his hold. Her knees touched on the soft pallet, her pussy poised and ready over Freyr's massive penis. With a gasp of pleasure and a sigh of relief, she slid the cock into her tingling receptacle. She felt her vagina stretch with the delicious pressure of his large organ. She guided him into her, feeling his cockhead press on her cervix and displaces her uterus upwards. After receiving the full length of his manhood inside, her buttocks rested now on his thighs. Reaching her hand behind her, she located the soft skin of his scrotum. She squeezed and fondled his orange-sized testicles, eliciting a murmur of pleasure from her virile fertility god.

She looked into the audience, reveled in this thrilling public exhibition of her powerful and wanton sexuality. She experienced their eyes scanning her sensuous curves and she knew their lust matched hers. She closed her eyes, sensing and feeling the sexual energy in the room, the liberation and primal power of her mind and soul to come and release. *This is my one and only opportunity to forge a crystal orb with exceptional power!* She remembered back to the moment. *There will be no second chances, and no going back.* Her efforts tonight to produce the final and irreversible payoff and spurred on by these thoughts, she concentrated and maximized her energy centers. *I will give this audience a performance they would never forget!* she resolved, as the excitement of her public exhibition filled her with lusty exuberance.

Her eyes opened and she looked one by one into the eyes of the crowd gathered around her. She ran her tongue over her lips and teeth with unhurried allure, arched her back, and settled her pussy onto the wizard's giant cock with provocative deliberation. She slowly undulated her hips with circular gyration, stimulating her g-spot with the rocking pressure of the rigid tool she moved inside her. She moaned, amazed by the incredible wetness that she felt now between her legs. Her dripping desire moistened the warlock's thighs as well. She slid her buttocks on the slippery puddle and lubricated her throbbing anus in the process.

She raised herself on his twelve-inch pole, removing the cock from her pussy momentarily. Glancing into the audience, she plunged the penis back inside her, crying out in pleasure as she did so. Up and down, she rode him with demonic frenzy. Her firm round tits shuddered and rippled with each down-stroke like two stranded jellyfish battered by the receding tide on a sandy beach. The slurping sound of the repetitive vaginal penetration filled the thirsty ears of the assembled listeners, echoing wetly through the granite cavern. Mahrea laughed to herself, deciding it was time to intensify her performance.

"Fuck me, pagan gods!" she screamed. "I want cock in my ass, mouth, and pussy!"

She reached for Odin, whose rock-hard erection only inches from her mouth. *He is the one I desire*, she acknowledged. *His face is disguised, but I know it is he.*

"Aaric the Supreme," she whispered his identity to herself. *The mysterious leader of their coven, the great and unapproachable dark wizard.* He quietly acknowledged her accurate recognition with a subtle nod.

She grasped his thirteen-inch penis, pulled it towards her eager moistened lips. She licked the undersurface of his cock, ran her tongue into the crevice joining his shaft to the head. Moving upwards, she found the fish-like mouth of his gigantic organ. Inserting the tip of her tongue into his penile orifice, she heard him moan as she circled the opening and inserted her talented oral appendage into his gaping channel. With a lascivious glimmer in her eye, she paused momentarily before she took the full length of his masculinity into her anxiously waiting oral cavity.

"I want your cum in my mouth!" she hissed, her husky voice echoing softly in the torch-lit cavern. "Help me forge my crystal, most powerful Odin, with your unrivaled release. I will use your jism for this... my most ambitious purpose."

On his knees beside her, he pushed his penis into her mouth. She gladly took it all, feeling the tense bulb of his aroused manhood pushing against the yielding softness of her tonsils and throat. She lay on Freyr's chest, her tits pushed against his well-developed torso and his cock submerged deep inside her pelvis. Her buttocks raised, ready for Thor who positioned his eleven-inch phallus on the wrinkled tightness of her pulsing anus.

Her hungry mouth filled with the savory meat of Odin's bulky and satisfying cock, which muffled her guttural cry of surprise and pleasure as Thor's cock slid smoothly into her anal canal. Her posterior entrance thoroughly lubricated, not only from the copious pilfered river of gushing desire emanated from her adjacent vagina, but also from its own slick excitement which oozed from tiny invisible pores in the pink and silky lining of her tightly puckered corridor. Thor's access was slippery and unhindered. He slid the full length of his organ into the tight ravine between her buttocks, penetrating her posterior orifice, a warrior's spear sinking into the flesh of his willing prey. *Oh, such excruciating pleasure*, she acknowledged. Her sphincter, stretched by the large cock submerged to the hilt in her anus, tingled with excitement as it gratefully dilated to accommodate the thickness of the welcome intruder.

The taste of Odin's musky manhood in her mouth, the feel of two cocks inside her, and the thrill of her eager and sexy public deflowering combined together to ignite the fuse of her ecstasy. Her release built and the time came. She must coordinate the physical and the metaphysical, directing her energy with theirs to create her powerful orb.

She temporarily extracted Odin's cock from her mouth to speak. "Fuck me hard, all three," she commanded. "My ecstasy draws near and we must come together. Great master," she cried, calling her instructions to the warlock disguised as Odin, "you are the keeper of my energy. Make me a crystal with my channeled power, combined with yours!"

Odin's cock slipped back in her mouth. She encircled his penis with the tightness of her damp lips, holding the base with both hands while she moved it in and out, moaning. He assisted her efforts, fucking her mouth like it was her pussy.

Looking up, she saw he extended his arms. His palms cupped together as if he held an invisible object. She smiled, knowing momentarily her crystal would materialize in that very spot, at the precise moment of her shattering orgasm.

Thor's cock slid in and out of her anus, while Freyr's penis pounded her cunt with the force of a jackhammer. Her release would come quickly, she recognized. She felt the pleasure gathering in her loins, her pussy a rain cloud humid with heavy wetness and ready to burst. And then, with the abruptness of a lightning storm, the torrential precipitation began.

She grasped Odin's penis tightly, extracting it from her mouth but resting the purple bulb of his massive arousal against her lips. "In Hecate's name," she gasped, "I command you to come with me now, all three. Come in my pussy, my ass, and my mouth!" she ordered.

Odin's cock was slick with her saliva. She circled it with her fist, using her hand to stimulate him while her tongue swirled around his opening and her lips touched his cockhead with expectant anticipation. Her pelvis felt as if it were a field of a thousand orchids, whose flowers all blossomed simultaneously.

She yelled out as the wetness in her loins squirted from her contracting pussy. "I'm coming!" she announced, although none misinterpreted the spraying geyser of ejaculation emanated from her luscious cunt. "My energy has now been released! Waste it not, my warlock partners!" she screamed.

Her body shook with the intensity of her climax and at that very moment, she felt the warm gush of jism in her anus and in her pussy. The two cocks below and behind pumped wildly with the force of their orgasms, as Odin's organ too, began to quiver.

She gripped Odin's cock tightly, bracing for the imminent illustration of his potent virility. Then - abruptly and violently - the creamy stream of his cum exploded in her mouth, filling her oral cavity with a viscous pool of the warlock's fertile masculinity. As his cum slithered from her lips, she licked the residual ooze from his still pulsing organ, swallowing every ounce of his salty jism with lusty triumph.

She looked at Odin's hands with nervous expectation and her heart pounded joyfully when she saw what he held. A swirling mass of vapor tumbled in his hands, rich with a kaleidoscope of colors. The gaseous cloud converged into the center of Odin's outstretched palms, concentrating itself into a shining orb the size of a large orange.

Curiously, a hazy bubble formed itself around the mass of energy, surrounding the vapor with a tenuous appearing film of dripping wetness. *This temporary casing is their combined ejaculate!* she realized with amazement. The vapor contained within, of her primal and psychic energy combined with theirs. Like the seafoam born from Ouranos's severed genitals, from which arose the vain and beautiful Aphrodite, their potent jism provided the shell of protection as well as the seed of life for her most powerful energy crystal.

Mahrea, preoccupied and intrigued by the evolving process, did not notice the transformation at first. The shell of ejaculate hardened, taking on the translucent appearance of frosty ice. Then, with a deafening roar and a blinding flash of light, the icy exterior replaced with a glimmering sphere of glass.

Her globe forged and she was quite pleased.

***

Mahrea stood in front of the mirror, smiled as she reviewed the events of that unforgettable initiation day. In comparison, everything else in her life seemed meaningless and trivial compared with her incredible orgy and the crystal orb it produced.

She scoffed, thinking of her new-born daughter with contempt. *What a useless waste of nine months,* she thought with frustration. "Dear, sweet Niamh," she said out loud with derision, mimicking the intonation and articulation of Rhys' voice. The child would be just like her father, the globe said and it never lied. *Kind, generous, and noble,* she thought distastefully. Attributes which never served the higher Wiccan purpose to which she so completely devoted her life. *The child is vacant,* the globe whispered in her head, the voice identical to her own. *Hers is a bland human core, devoid of magic or power, so waste not your time on her, sweet mistress!* her alter ego advised.

But the boy, she thought sadly. He would have been a great warlock or so her crystal told her. *No matter now*, she concluded. She would accept Hecate's fateful decision and do now should be done. *There will be another son,* she told herself with reassuring confidence. After all, the globe prophesied a warlock heir and the crystal always knew. *There is no alternative; I will simply have to bed him again, and as soon as possible!* She decided, thinking with distaste of her Gaelic husband.

She shrugged, admiring the smooth slope of her beautiful shoulders and the delicate ridge of her perfect clavicles. *He will be an easy mark!* she sniggered. She severed their sexual relations as soon his seed planted and she knew he would be exceedingly pliable after nine months of frustrating abstinence. She moved her hands to her breasts again, pushed them together to accentuate their full and rounded perfection. *Who wouldn't lust for my attentions?* she asked herself with a seductive smile. *There is no man in this kingdom or any other, for that matter, who would turn down a chance to fuck this extraordinary body, if only once!*

She walked to her bed, picked up the orb from its resting place under her pillow. *It is time to consult my counselor again,* she reflected as she gazed deeply into the sphere of concentrated energy.

As customary, the hypnotic pull from the extension of her metaphysical psyche was immediate and intense. The sucking vortex of the orb drew her in. In an instant, she immersed in the all-consuming energy of the sphere's vastness, separate yet integrated, like a diver surrounded by the alien yet familiar surroundings of a favorite ocean haunt. Drowning in the promise of all-seeing clairvoyance and dizzy with the power that surged through her soul, she held her breath, dived deeply and eagerly into the glittering crystal.

***

The globe took her back in time, to the day of her arrival at Dunscaith.

A handful of her family's servants traveled with her post-marital journey across the North Atlantic, but they returned home shortly on the same vessel that had carried them from Vik on the southern Icelandic coast, across the waters to Port Righ on Skye.

She and the Gaelic warlord wed in a quiet ceremony in Isafjordhur and afterwards, her new husband traveled ahead to prepare his castle for her arrival. Two months later, she arrived and reunited with the commonplace man she equated with a tedious obligation. *I should have been promised to the great Aaric,* she thought. *Our combined powers could have equaled those of the powerful Hecate herself,* she pondered sadly. She remembered the feel of his cock in her throat and the taste of his cum on her lips. *Alas, a permanent union between us will never come to pass,* she sighed. But ah, the sweet memory of his potent manhood, crucial in the making of her crystal, stayed with her.

Rhys dispatched a dozen of his soldiers to greet her and three hours later the party finally neared Dunscaith. The sun setting and the shadow of the looming fortress poured like a dark and elongated stream from an invisible well at the castle's base. The dark granite structure blended into the bleakness of its own shadow, giving an eerie illusion of continuity. The black extension of the stone monolith seemed to stretch endlessly across the rocky causeway and onto the green and hilly carpet of the surrounding countryside, reaching towards the approaching traveling party like an arm that warned and threatened. The spiraling towers and jutting turrets formed jagged and bony fingers on a claw-like hand, but these insignificant digits protruded from the castle's outstretched and beckoning appendage. The castle's tower spiraled above its diminutive counterparts like Kronos before his fall, remained as the last surviving descendant of Gaia before his overthrow by his own son Zeus. She looked thoughtfully at the jutting tower which brought to mind a gigantic deity of a quite different variety. She smiled knowingly, remembering the firm and rigid bulk of Aaric's massive phallus she grasped that night in her hungry hands.

The intimidating specter of the ominous fortress appealed to her dark soul. The threat of retribution lurked in its shadow and the unseen chains of regret and sorrow clung tightly to its grey and weeping facade. She clutched her globe tightly under her cloak, feeling the reassurance of its solid and compact weight in her hand and the promise of its concentrated power tingling on her palm. *Yes*, she confirmed, *the orb knows. This place cannot conceal its pain from my crystal's discerning eye.*

She turned brusquely to the lieutenant that rode by her side. "Warrior," she queried with a condescending smile on her face. "Have you a name?"

"Caedmon, Mistress," he replied tersely. His face wore the stony expressionless look of a professional soldier, but underneath his impassive facade she sensed his discomfort. *Good*, she thought, pleased to discern the underlying uneasiness would certainly assist in giving her the upper hand.

"Caedmon," she began, gazed distractedly at the rigid appendage emerged organ-like from the castle's body. "This spiraling tower intrigues me. Is it used for a lookout, or for some other secret purpose?"

"The battlements provide a sweeping view, Mistress," he replied tensely. "From that vantage point, we can easily spot an enemy's approach from a five mile distance surrounding us."

He was silent, awkwardly awaited her response. She savored the tense atmosphere for a moment, before continuing her interrogation.

"The tower," she prompted. "Explain the reason, loyal lieutenant, for this unnecessary erection."

Caedmon shrugged nervously, unsure of her intention in pursuing this unusual line of questioning. "Our Thane ordered its construction when he commissioned the builders," he said. "His vision reaches now to the heavens, for all to see."

She nodded. "It has piqued my interest," she stated. "Is there a room at the top I could inhabit?" she asked.

"There is a room," Caedmon confirmed, "but it is our Thane's private sanctuary."

"Ah, what a shame," she said, her voice laced with light sarcasm. "I would have been quite comfortable in the vulture's lofty nest."

Caedmon frowned. Uncomfortable with her choice of words, he struggled to grasp the significance of her peculiar choice of imagery.

"Rhys spends much of his time in his eagle's aery," he retorted, emphasizing his own avian simile. "Worry not, Lady," he said with caustic reassurance. "We have prepared a luxurious suite of rooms for you in the east wing. You will be quite comfortable and satisfied with your accommodations, I am sure!"

They rode the remaining distance in silence. *This tower will play some role in my evil task here*, she thought sure of this.

Night fell as they reached the castle. The gates opened, the drawbridge down, and their way prepared. She arrived.

***

She sat at a small but luxuriously appointed table with Rhys at her one side and Caedmon on the other, at the far side of the banquet hall. Perpendicular to theirs and running the entire length of the fifty-foot room, were aligned a single column of tables in head to head sequence, overflowing with victuals and refreshments. The room buzzed with activity, as countless servants attended to the demands and needs of over one hundred guests at the welcome reception.

"The people of Skye anxiously awaited your arrival," Caedmon said. "They love their thane dearly," he explained, avoiding her gaze, "and wish nothing more for him than happiness."

He is subtle in his insolence, she thought. *He knows full well I have no concern for the peasants in this foreign land, nor do I care about the happiness of my pitiful husband. Aaric urged her to marry the Gael as a means to an end.* Her sinister purpose finally revealed. Before the banquet, she enjoyed mental communion with her globe, learning her union with the foreign warlord would produce a son whose supernatural talents would match or exceed her own. Her heart beat quickly with excitement, now the orb clarified her mission. She must bed her new husband tonight and every night, until her belly swelled with the fullness of his child. The globe did not lie and its prophecy she must fulfill.

Caedmon awaited her response, but she wielded the unspoken weapon of silence for a moment longer. She raised her glass slowly, sipped her wine with measured leisure. Finally, she opened her mouth to speak, stifling a yawn as she did so. "And why, pray tell, do these lowly people love him so?" She directed her question to the lieutenant, intentionally ignoring Rhys who sat right beside her.

"Rhys is kind and fair, but he is also a fearsome warrior and a powerful leader. He protects them, and rules with an even and just hand. Why should they not love him?" Caedmon, prepared with his answer, did not hesitate.

His rhetorical question required no answer, she decided. Mahrea drank quietly from her cup as Rhys acknowledged the compliment.

"Thank you, Caedmon," he said. "A more loyal friend and lieutenant exist not in all of Skye and the Isles."

Mahrea gazed at Rhys with a mixture of curiosity and contempt. *He is certainly handsome,* she thought, *but his kind and forgiving spirit detracts greatly from his appeal. What a striking contrast,* she reflected, *between this useless nobleman and the dark danger of a man like Aaric. But this potent Gaelic cock might still please and perform!* she contemplated. After all, she should try to make the most of things. Since his penis had a momentous duty to perform in her pussy and she had no choice in the selection, she might as well enjoy the meat he must thrust inside her!

She looked casually around the banquet hall, studying the guests busy eating at the tables and the servers who attended them. One of the servants, for no reason in particular, caught her attention. The girl's skin seemed unusually ruddy as if darkened intentionally with an extract or a dye. Her hair also lightened, it seemed and as she bent over to retrieve a platter of meat from a portly nobleman, Mahrea glimpsed some padding underneath the girl's blouse. *Undoubtedly placed there,* Mahrea concluded, *to give the false impression of girth.*

The girl looked towards the head table and for a brief moment their eyes locked. Mahrea glared back, focusing all of her malignant arrogance and spite into her gaze. *What fun*, she sneered. *These insignificant insects must learn to fear me and I will start with this meaningless peasant girl.*

It took but a brief moment for her transmission to be received. The servant girl shuddered, her eyes wide as she recognized Mahrea's hatred. The girl looked away, shaking with fear. She nervously gathered the platter and retreated into the safety of the kitchen.

Mahrea smiled, pleased by the potency of her contact spell. The interaction over and, without another thought for the servant girl, she turned her attention back to her untouched meal.

But wait, the globe showed her more! The servant was back in the banquet hall and the orb showed her face in profile. Turning, her eyes shone with bright and happy recognition. She looked at someone and her face beamed with the hot fire of desire, yearning, and love.

This scene deviated from the script of Mahrea's actual experience. Her contact with the girl ended immediately after Mahrea cast her visual touching spell. *So why are you showing me this, crystals?* Mahrea wondered. "Explain," she demanded out loud, addressing her alter ego. "Why show me this insignificant girl, orb?"

The crystal was silent and Mahrea drew the obvious conclusion. "This girl will play some role in my drama," she stated, certain of the globe's intention. "Show me more, crystal sphere."

The orb's narrative continued. Curiously, the maiden overly preoccupied with the front table, despite her silent and frightening confrontation a moment ago with Mahrea. *Does she not fear the threat of meeting my gaze again?* Mahrea asked herself incredulously. *Such bravery is inspiring, but foolish,* she mused.

Mahrea, with analytical interest, attempted to determine the maiden's purpose. *Does she lust for the lieutenant?* the sorceress asked herself. *No,* she concluded, *she must have her eye on one of the Thane's attendants.*

Now the orb showed Rhys, who finished his meal, engaged in conversation with a landholder. As he chatted with the nobleman, his eyes casually scanned the gathering, perhaps to confirm his guests satisfied with the food and drink.

Suddenly, he froze in his place as the sunrise of recognition dawned on his face. *He has seen the lady in disguise and he knows her!* Mahrea realized suddenly. Rhys raised his hand, attempting to catch the girl's attention, but instead of calling her to him, his gesture had the opposite effect. The girl looked alarmed, immediately cleared her table in haste before rushing out of the room.

They were lovers, but no longer, Mahrea recognized with shock. But why would her globe show her this vision, unless it had some relevance to her present situation?

At the moment this question passed through her mind, the scene abruptly changed. Mahrea no longer relived her welcome banquet. Instead, she was a silent and invisible observer in her husband's bedchamber. Naked Rhys engaged in sexual relations with a dark-haired, fair-skinned beauty in front of the fireplace. The woman, on her hands and knees, panted in the throes of passion while Rhys fucked her vigorously from behind. The maiden cried out as her body shook with the intensity of a powerful orgasm.

It only took Mahrea a moment to process what she saw. In a flash, she knew.

"It's her!" she whispered to the globe. "It's the maiden from the banquet!"

"Yes," the crystal audibly hissed. "Beware, Enchantress. She will sabotage your plans unless you stop her."

Mahrea felt the anger seething in her spleen. "This scene you show..." she asked, "is it yet to be or is it a vision from my pitiful husband's past?"

The orb laughed. "Mistress," it sneered, "your husband lies with her at this very moment! This scene takes place now, in this same castle, in the very bedroom where you yourself used his cock for your own sinister purpose!"

Dizzy with rage, she violently shook off the orb's spell, withdrawing herself from her hypnotic trance like a dreamer willing herself to wake from a terrible nightmare. The crystal shimmered with derision as it in lay in her hand at her side. She impatiently slid it under her pillow, preoccupied with the information she learned and her intent on destroying her newfound enemy.

She stood, paced back and forth in front of the mirror. Her head pounded and throbbed with searing hatred for the woman who dared to interfere with her awesome and predetermined destiny. The acrid bile of her spiteful anger burned in her throat.

"The insolence and stupidity of this maiden astounds me," she muttered under her breath. "She shall pay with her life," she pledged in front of the mirror. She gazed at her own reflection with the detached curiosity of a heartless assassin, noticing with satisfaction the unmistakable glint of brutal vengefulness glimmering in the cold and icy grey eyes staring back at her.

"All three shall suffer," she concluded out loud. The girl she decided to kill, when the time was right. *And the baby?* "She shall die too," she announced to the empty room. The child, devoid of occult talent, served no useful purpose. *This so-called daughter of mine will only complicate matters further with the passage of time and thus, her life I will end!* she concluded with evil determination.

"But Rhys," she said to her listening reflection, "he shall live!"

A more perfect punishment she could not imagine. *Oh, the excruciating heartache he will feel and the joyful redemption I will enjoy!* she thought excitedly. *His daughter and his lover, both dead - and only himself to blame! Oh, such intense sorrow and regret he will feel and all of this, produced solely by his weak and naive kindness and his sickening belief in the power of love.*

"He will live a long and tortured life," she said out loud. "As Hecate is my evil mistress, he will live to regret and despise the foolish and irrevocable errors made by his pure and nostalgic romantic soul."

Chapter Eight
Gwenhwyvar

Gwen rested in Rhys' arms, enjoying the ruddy glow from her subsiding second climax, which warmed her face with more satisfying intensity than the pulsing embers of the quickly dying fire. He found sleep almost immediately, spent and content after his purging release. She smiled, feeling the evidence of months, or maybe even years of his constrained frustration, drip and ooze from her happily violated orifice.

She gently disengaged herself from his loving embrace, careful not to disturb him as she quietly stood. Laying some logs on the fire, she watched as the dry and brittle wood quickly took flame, sudden and instantaneous, like the magical result of some magician's trick. She hugged her knees, sitting peacefully now at his side as she watched the slow repetitive rise and fall of his broad and muscular chest.

She hardly believed she was here with him. Her place, she knew, was at his side, but until today, she gave up hope she would ever feel his gentle touch or enjoy his rigid cock again. Her heart fluttered in her chest as she remembered the touch of his lips and tongue on her clit, his hands and fingers on her tits. "Oh, I have missed you so, my only lover," she said to him softly, laying her hand tenderly on his toned and well-developed chest.

What would they do now, she wondered? He loved her, she knew, but what about his matrimonial mistress, to whom he pledged his unwilling heart in obedient resignation, bound to her by duty and by political allegiance but not by love? He would not be able to cast her off like a piece of armor that did not and would never fit properly after all; it was fashioned with someone else entirely in mind. And even if it was possible to annul the union, such a divorce would greatly anger her Viking kin and in so doing threaten the peace and safety of the entire Isle.

And what if the rumors were true? She felt the cold and evil power of the Nordic princess in her gaze that night when their eyes locked momentarily across the busy banquet hall. Gwen remembered that moment with a shudder. Mahrea's icy stare reached deeply into Gwen's soul, gripping her kind spirit in a stranglehold threatening to kill and destroy. It employed all of Gwen's strength of will to look away and somehow she knew if she had not broken the spell of engagement, the tightening hand of the witch's malice around her heart would have ended her life right then and there.

Gwen had little doubt Mahrea was well practiced in the dark arts. How else could a single look transmit such physical impact, if not accompanied by an enchanter's spell or a sorcerer's curse? Suddenly, the implications of such a reality sliced into her consciousness like a dagger, ripping open the curtains of her vulnerability with brutal and jolting abruptness. Her ears pulsed with her panicked heartbeat, fueled by the adrenaline rush of fear the recognition of danger pumped into her veins. *She will kill me with some unworldly spell!* she realized. Her mind raced. Rhys, valiant and brave, would undoubtedly rush to her aid, but his sword and shield powerless weapons in such an otherworldly conflict.

She calmed herself, slowed her heartbeat by sheer force of will. *God will give me strength, and the goodness of our love will prevail,* she thought, as peaceful reassurance embraced her like a mother's arms.

Rhys stirred on the carpet beside her, shifting himself in his sleep so that his arm rested in her lap. She took his hand, raised it to her lips with tender and heartfelt gratitude. "I adore you," she whispered, pledging she would suffer nothing short of the tortures of hell to regain his love. She smiled at the irony, since she might in fact have to do just that.

She closed her eyes, clutching her lover's hand tightly as she wept her warm tears of sadness and joy, both. "Oh sweet Orpheus," she said, "I am your Eurydice. If you succeed in bargaining with Hades, please lead me safely from the Underworld and into your loving, welcoming arms!"

At the sound of her voice, he stirred again and opened his eyes.

"What upset you, sweet lover?" he asked, raising himself into a sitting position and taking her into his arms. He brushed the tears from her eyes, kissing her on each cheek as he did so.

She shook her head. "I am fine, Rhys. We should rest now and talk later."

Rising, she pulled him onto his feet and led him towards the soft downy comfort of the enormous feather bed. They climbed in together, joined as one under the warm comforter as they held each other in a tight and tender embrace.

Slumber found Rhys hurriedly. She lay in his arms, her mind frantically active as she tried to process the life changing events of the past day, months, and years. She would sleep soon enough, but now, she retired to the private spot in her heart and attempted to reconcile her sorrow with her happiness.

***

Slightly over two years, twenty-seven months, to be exact, since they last been together last. She remembered the day as if it happened yesterday. Every detail etched in her memory, like an intricate painting whose every brushstroke formed a lasting and unforgettable impression on its awestruck viewer. His offhand gestures, the subtle curve of his smile and the endearing inflections of his voice: all of these images indelibly imprinted on the cellophane film reel of her mind poised for playback at a moment's notice.

She sighed, recalling their last intimate encounter with nostalgia. Neither of them knew this meeting would be their last. Although she knew of his summoning to conference with the King of Mann, she never dreamed the consultation's repercussions on their relationship. They both assumed Olaf planned some military offensive, for which he needed support and assistance. As the Thane of Skye and a member of the war council for the Hebrides, only be natural for Rhys to be included in preliminary discussions and preparations for battle.

Such heavenly bliss enjoyed that day, followed by such poignant heartbreak and emotional pain later. Her mind was a marathon runner fueled by an endorphin high and she simply could not stop the relentless pace of her ceaseless thoughts. She relived the day now as she lay sleepless next to the man she thought she lost forever.

The early autumn nights were cool, but the days still warm. She awoke that morning thinking of him as customary, but her longing for his touch and the feel of his body pressed against hers more intense than usual, since more than a week passed without a sign or word from him. Oh, how she desired him, body and soul. She prayed he might send or call for her soon. She needed his physical closeness to satisfy her burning obsession for his love.

Their romance had been a quiet affair, by necessity. Her parents, aware of her clandestine and carnal dalliances with the handsome Thane, were naturally concerned for her reputation and sensitive to the social repercussions she undoubtedly faced if her indiscretions with Rhys discovered, they honored her privacy by maintaining a sacred oath of silence.

Her meetings with her lover always cloaked in secrecy. Rhys' trusted and loyal lieutenant, Caedmon, sometimes whisked her away in the dead of night or as was more often the case, Rhys appeared unannounced and without warning, his appearance disguised so he remained unrecognized as the just and powerful Lord of Skye. They would discreetly retreat together to some private location and enjoy the beauty of their mutual physical passion or he would carry her off on horseback to a distant inn or tavern, where they would slyly play the role of husband and wife to the unsuspecting innkeeper. So many trysts, so many journeys and so many passionate nights spent together as furtive and covert lovers. Although the adventures were rich and exciting, she longed for the day when their relationship could be open and transparent rather than secretive and hidden. If he someday took her as his wife rather than keep her as a mistress, she would gladly become his devoted and loving partner as well as a permanently satisfying and seductive sexual prize.

As she rose from her cot in the corner of the cottage, she stretched her limber and sexy body by arching her back with her arms behind her head. Her parents and brother already risen, probably shortly before dawn, to get an early start on the long day's work ahead, Aillyn still sound asleep in her bed. Gwen pulled off her nightshirt, enjoying the feel of the cool air on her luscious naked skin. Touching her breasts, she felt the hard pebble of her aroused nipples under her fingertips. *I am in dire need*, she laughed to herself. She hoped Rhys came soon.

She pulled a light cotton dress over her head, smoothing the fabric over her tingling and needful body. Aillyn stirred in her bed, awakened by the sound of her sister's preparations.

"Where go you, Sister?" she inquired, raising herself up on one elbow while she rubbed the remnant of sleep from her rich brown eyes.

"To tend the chickens," she replied. "There is much to do today, Aillyn and I will have need of your help later but now you may rest," she said kindly.

"I will rise, Sister," Aillyn said with a yawn. "The sooner my chores are finished, the sooner I can meet sweet Colum."

Aillyn had been seeing a local townsman's son who seemed more serious about the relationship than her sister. Gwen's suspicion Aillyn's main interest in the lad involved the large size of his cock, judging from the descriptions she heard from her lusty sibling.

Gwen, heading for the door, called back to her sister. "Take the extract given to you by old woman Rhoswen, Lass," she reminded. "Lie with sweet strapping Colum if you please, but let not his virile seed take hold in your unwed womb!"

Placing her hand on the handle, she pushed the door open. It was a beautiful morning, unseasonably warm for the time of year. Her mother fetched some water at the well the morning wash.

"Morning, Ma!" she called, making her way across the courtyard towards the henhouse.

"Morning, dear one," her mother replied. "Come here for a moment, Lass and help me with this heavy bucket.

Her mother lowered the largest pail into the spring and struggled now to haul it over the lip of the stone well. Much of the water splashed out of the wooden container as she struggled with the unexpected weight.

Gwen laughed. "Will you never learn, Ma?" she asked. "The large pail is for Da'. You have not the strength to manage the weight of it!"

"Stop your chiding, Girl," her mother said with feigned irritation. "Come now, before I fall in!"

Gwen smiled, amused by her mother's stubborn resolution and her good-natured disposition. "I guess the chickens can wait," she said, hoping to incite some more playful banter with her nonchalance. In no great hurry, being convinced that her mother had exaggerated her supplications, she steered a leisurely course across the courtyard towards the well in answer to her mother's overstated entreaties.

But before she covered even half the distance, her mother lost her grip on the bucket, lurched forward in a valiant attempt to retrieve the swaying pail. Determined to prevail against her smug opponent, she stretched her arms outward, balancing her top-heavy frame precariously on the rim of the wall. With horror, Gwen saw the scene in slow motion. In a moment, her mother's balance escaped her and kicked her legs furiously to counteract the inescapable pull of gravity, and aimed head first into the deep and algae coated abyss.

Gwen blinked her eyes, unwilling to accept the reality of what she witnessed. As if conjured from thin air, a cloaked figure appeared behind the falling matriarch. Concealed in the dense wooded brush that grew by the side of the cottage, he emerged as a grateful answer to their dire need at the most critical moment. His arms around her waist, he pulled her decisively away from the hole and onto the dusty ground on top of him.

Gwen was at their side a moment later, helping her startled and flustered mother to her feet. After tending first to the defeated homemaker, she planned to turn her attentions to the Good Samaritan.

"Are you all right, Ma'?" she asked, looking her up and down to satisfy herself there were no serious injuries.

"I am fine, Daughter," her mother replied, flushed with self-conscious embarrassment. "Help me with the poor gentleman, Gwen. I hope I have not hurt him."

Gwen took his hand, which felt strangely familiar. Her heart skipped a beat. Looking down at the smiling face of the mysterious rescuer, she saw immediately it was Rhys.

His face disguised by a week's bearded stubble, enhanced with the grey and shadowy smudges of a fireplace coal. He wore a green hood, which shielded his face and covered his head as an effective visual deterrent if any should attempt to scrutinize his features. He stood and after making sure they had no audience, save for Gwen's flabbergasted mother, he took his lover in his arms and kissed her deeply.

"I missed you so," he said. "Come with me, Gwen. I have a special destination in mind!"

And a moment later, she sat behind him on a galloping grey steed, her heart in his hands as they began another carnal adventure which proved to be their last.

***

They rode for hours, finally arriving at a small lakeside cottage on the far side of Skye. The late afternoon sun cast its warm but waning autumn brilliance onto the surface of the calm water like a softly burning torch whose wick was quickly drying. The shepherd's hut rested comfortably at the edge of the Loch, cradled in the safe embrace of a wooded conifer enclave. The rocky beach at the water's edge bravely held its thin line of defense against the soft carpet of pine needles that dominated the local terrain.

She took in the peaceful surroundings, as Rhys led the horse to the water's edge, letting him drink his fill. Afterwards, he led the steed to a small grassy patch of ground to feed, tying the reigns loosely to a tree stump before leaving the animal to enjoy his dinner and a good night's rest.

"This place is beautiful," she commented softly.

He nodded, acknowledging the seemingly endless expanse of water that stretched before them. "Loch Eynort," he said quietly. "This spot is very dear to my heart.

He piqued her curiosity. "Why, Rhys?" she asked, touching his face lightly with her hand.

He sighed. "When I was but a lad," he explained, "my Da' would take me here." He paused, his eyes searching the horizon sadly. "We would fish and he shared his stories with me." His eyes teared. "I miss him dearly."

She took his face in her hands, kissed his cheeks with tender consolation. He looked out at the water. She followed his gaze, half-expecting to actually see his father in the distance reclining in a fishing boat or wading in the shallows with net in hand.

"This cottage," she asked, "did it belong to him?"

He shook his head. "Abandoned years ago, I have made it my own, though and I come here often to be alone."

He looked at her now, his hazel eyes melting her heart with their warm richness. "Dear sweet Gwen," he said, "I have shared this place with no one. But now I share it with you and you alone!"

Her heart thumped in her throat. *Oh, how I love him*, she sighed. *He is my life, and my soul!* Her desire for him burned in the hearth of her pussy, like Hestia's hot and immortal Olympian flame.

Looking around, she confirmed their solitude. "Oh I need you so, Rhys," she panted, pulling her dress over her head, and swiftly stepping out of her sandals. She stood before him, nude and glorious, her incomparable beauty exposed to any might be secretly observing. She walked over to him, took his hand, and guided it to her slick and yearning pussy. He gasped, surprised at the extent of her fast arousal.

She leaned forward, pushing her tits against him, and whispering in his ear. "I want you, Rhys, right here and now!" Her tongue drifted in his ear, probing deeply with moist and diligent expertise.

His breath quickened. "Inside, perhaps," he managed to suggest.

She shook her head, leading him away from the cottage and towards the rocky shore, pushing him onto a bed of pine needles in a small clearing on the edge of the tree line. With a seductive laugh, she started undressing him.

He looked stunned. "But..." he started.

She placed her fingers gently on his lips, silencing him with her touch. "If there are witnesses, so be it!" she declared. "I will never love any man but you and I want the world to know."

He smiled, looking as if he had a secret he wished to share. "What is it, Rhys?" she asked.

He shook his head. "Not now," he said. "I have made a decision, but it is not yet time to share it with you."

Her face flushed with excitement. *Perhaps he plans to make me a different sort of mistress!* she silently hoped. She enjoyed the fantasy of this thought for a moment as she continued undressing him. Oh, how she longed to share in his life, in his bed and at his side as the honest and legitimate Lady of Dunscaith and Mistress of Skye.

The promise of commitment and the hope the secrecy might soon end fueled her craving for uninhibited and public intimacy. With bold determination, she voraciously and forcefully ripped the tunic from his torso, hurriedly exposing the tense and lean muscles of his warrior's chest. She looked at him hungrily, turning her attentions now to the bulge in his leggings. With avid determination, she slipped off his buckskin trews, tossed them aside with the remnants of his shirt.

He is incredibly beautiful, she thought, admiring the well-defined lines of his flawless physique and the rigid sleekness of his impressive ten-inch organ. He shifted towards her slightly which pressed his cock suggestively onto the smooth curve of her nude waist. No longer hesitant, his body language begged for her lusty attention: unconcealed, uninhibited, and unconstrained.

"Let them watch," he panted, looking with excitement now to the right and to the left along the pebble-strewn shoreline. "If there are spies, they are more than welcome to observe and witness their Thane's ecstasy with his one and only love and mistress."

She seductively stretched her trim and curvaceous body lengthwise, her left side on the bed of pine needles and her right side pressed lightly against his side. Bending her right leg over his supine form, she prepared to pull herself on top of him, face-to-face for the delicious execution of her happy task. Smiling, he stopped her with his strong arms encircling her waist, gently encouraging a different position by redirecting her orientation.

Immediately understanding his silent request, she pivoted 180 degrees, swinging her left leg over his body instead of her right. Resting on top of him now in a sixty-nine position, she felt him pull her pussy thankfully onto his face, his oral lips on her feminine lips, his probing tongue on her eager labial flesh, his lubricating wetness making an unforgettable donation to the soaking secretions dripping from her sexy cunt.

She sat on his face, slowly grinding her aching slit onto the itching post of his unshaven cheeks and his chiseled jaw. She maneuvered her clit directly over the expert stimulation of his tongue, lying flat on his chest and stomach as she grasped his cock with both hands. She rapidly flicked her tongue on the undersurface of his engorged glans, mimicking with identical precision the oral stimulation he joyfully inflicted on her tingling clitoris at the exact same moment. She was consumed with a pure animal lust seeming to intensify as she slipped his entire ten-inches into her ravenous mouth. The feel of his bulk in her hungry orifice triggered a surge of warm moisture between her legs, which she avidly smeared on his industrious lips with a muffled laugh.

His thrusting hips told the story of his own urgent needs. While the reality of his rigid desire filled her oral cavity, the concomitant certainty of her building release swelled in her loins. He flicked her clitoris with the tip of his tongue, while she frantically rubbed her burning labia and her pulsating anal dimple on his upper lip and nose. Her desire was a fiery sun, warming her pelvis with the searing radiant heat of a supernova soon to explode on his face. Her dwarf star, ignited its carbon fusion, neared its Chandrasekhar limit. In a moment, her runaway nuclear fusion unstoppable and would lead to a powerful galactic climax.

The taste of his pre-cum on her lips lit the atomic fuse of her celestial sphere. Her orgasm exploded inside her, sending waves of pleasure to all four corners of her body's universe. She removed his penis from her mouth, watching with excitement as a small preliminary stream of jism oozed from the gaping orifice of his barely twitching organ. Her body filled by the expanding stellar shockwave. The tingling electrons in her contracting pussy transmitted their radioactive intensity to every muscle and bone in her feminine solar system. *What an exquisite release,* she thought, as her lust-fueled heart pounded in her chest.

She preferred to have his cum inside her. She gently pinched the top of his glans, hoping this maneuver temporarily prevented a full-blown ejaculation. Her efforts successful, she licked the salty preamble from his organ as the twitching quickly subsided. "I want your cum inside me," she cried, her voice echoing across the deserted lake.

She urgently slid her soaking pussy across his chest and navel, raising herself on her haunches as her hands clutched both of his calves for support. She reached between her legs, grasping his penis and pulling it towards her. Having extended his rock hard organ to the limit, she poised his spearhead over her yearning target. She moved her labial lips aside, sinking his manhood into her feminine orifice like a piston rod pumping into an engine cylinder.

She gasped when she felt his bulk inside her, hoping his sexual accelerator flooded her engine with a second gushing fuel leak. "Fill me with your manhood, Rhys," she screamed, her voice reverberated across the peaceful lake and startling a flock of curlews feeding nearby on the shore. They flapped their wings in agitated annoyance, relocated to a safer and quieter location a few yards away.

He lifted his buttocks into the air, his cock penetrating forcefully into the depths of her pelvis. She suspended on the platform of his pubis, his penis inserted into the cul-de-sac behind her cervix like a snake nestled in an underground den. His serpent's desire pushed anxiously on the wall between her vagina and her rectum. She settled the cobra-like head into her cervical recess, grinding his one-eyed monster against the back of her uterus with a slow gyrating rotation of her hips. The exquisite pressure of his organ buried to the hilt in her pussy, would send her on a second journey into the realm of ecstasy. Her fuel cells, still warm from the slow burn of re-entry from her first orgasm, quickly reignited. She felt the missile of a second release being prepared for an uncontrollable take-off.

She slid her pussy wildly up and down on his penis like a persistent and determined traveler with stone and flint who hopes the resulting sparks will eventually light her dry tinder. She felt wild, free and exhilarated, exposed and vulnerable, yet safe and in control. She wanted her second release and it came now.

The powerful waterfall of her cum whose floodwaters surged over the edge of her vaginal precipice crashed and splashed onto the flat and level surface of his navel and groin. The volume of her ejaculate was truly startling. Each pumping vaginal spasm accompanied by a squirting stream of her liquid ecstasy, which rushed like a newly discovered oil deposit whose gushing rich crude successfully dredged by his penetrating excavation tool in her plentiful and saturated field of secretions. She shuddered as her ejaculate poured from the pores of her vagina, making his stomach slippery with her musky and aromatic sex.

With a groan of satisfaction, she straightened her back and shifted her hands, which she rested behind her, leaning backwards while supporting her weight on the ledge of his ribcage. She settled his cockhead into the crater of her cervical os, engaging his gun into the comfortable silky holster of her quivering womb. She was prepared for his powder to spark, anxious for the explosion propelling his lusty bullets into her waiting and eager receptacle. She rocked back and forth, agitating her cervix against the trigger point of his rigid barrel.

She glanced back, licking her lips seductively as she gazed into his intense hazel eyes. She sensed the imminent climax in his expression. He bit his lower lip, closed his eyes as his abdominal muscles became tense with the premonition of his ecstasy.

"Come now, Lover," she coaxed. "Fire your steaming load of cum into my pussy."

Her words were like the pull of a finger on his trigger. "My sweet, sweet lover," he cried out. "I'm coming now."

She felt his penis twitch wildly in her tight and accommodating canal. She felt the force of his ejaculate, first in her cervical canal and then at the back of her vagina as his cock danced uncontrollably in the tight and warm ballroom of her cunt. "My dear God in heaven," she screamed, amazed she actually experienced the power of his sexual explosion so deep in her pelvis. *So discreet, palpable, and tangible,* she thought, as real and concrete as the touch of his fingers on her skin or the feel of his lips kissing hers.

As his orgasm subsided, she felt his sexual moisture mixing with hers, one shared fluid, desire, and life for each other. She could not imagine being without him, and she knew he felt the same way. They were soul mates, twin flames - one person in two separate bodies. He was hers and she was his, now and forever.

***

They retired to the cottage, as the autumn sun began to set on the far side of the quiet lake. Lying together on a small cot in the corner, he held her in his arms, kissing her cheeks and stroking her dark hair as she dozed peacefully. She drifted in and out of a deep post-coital sleep when he finally spoke.

"I have been summoned to meet with the King of the Isles," he said quietly. Although his voice calm, she sensed a nervous apprehension in his tone atypical for the brave warlord.

She looked at him with concern. "Are there rumors of war?" she asked, unaware of any such talk in peasant circles.

He shook his head. "I have not heard of any plans for aggression," he replied, "although Olaf Godredsson is unpredictable, self-serving, and ambitious." He paused, appearing to ponder all of the potential motivations driving the Viking ruler's request to see him. "Olaf has close alliances with the kings of Ireland and Scotland," he commented, "and his rule over these western islands is undisputed. I cannot imagine he would jeopardize his uncontested power here with an invasion or an incursion onto the mainland. But anything is possible, especially when expansion and consolidation of his realm, separate and independent from Norway, always his unspoken goal."

She shuddered with dread. "If you are called away, my sweet, I will simply die!"

He touched her face with gentle hands. "Ne'er you worry, my darling. I will return to you always... even if I should die."

"No talk of death," she chided, crossing herself with superstitious alarm. "If you should die, I would take my own life in order to join you in eternity."

He kissed her deeply and when their kiss ended, he closed his eyes, the weary lines of worry and fatigue apparent on his handsome brow.

Although he slept, she could not. She lied awake the rest of the night, restless and apprehensive about the summons from the Viking king.

***

They rode back in silence the next morning. He said his goodbyes and her tears flowed freely as she watched him leave. "I will love you, forever," she said quietly, as horse and rider disappeared over the hill at the edge of town.

A week later, when she received his letter shattering her world and decimating all hope her life worth living.

***

Her memories of their final meeting and her subsequent heartbreak faded, much like the mist of sleep that shortly blanketed her consciousness with the soft cover of oblivion and nothingness. She slept deeply for a time, but became restless again. Was she awake or sleeping? *So hard to discriminate*, she thought, until the dream began.

So vivid, yet so confusing. The images come in fragments and snatches, like fleeting glimpses of an elusive sea creature surfacing periodically to briefly announce the unmistakable reality of its existence, only to submerge itself again into the dark cover and obscurity of its deep and mysterious watery home.

The waves crash behind her as she stands on the rock-strewn beach facing a steep sheer cliff. A granite fortress of a castle, essentially the one and same graced with grey boulders and rocks. Looking up, she notices the sky, an identical dismal and granite grey, blending seamlessly with the outline of the stronghold, thus giving the impression the cliff, bastion, and cloudy atmosphere all the same entity.

This is Dunscaith, her subconscious states, yet, it isn't. So familiar but simultaneously foreign, like a former lover from decades earlier whose appearance became shockingly altered with the cruel passage of time, barely recognizable, yet retaining a subtle hint of the long forgotten features of youth. She strains her neck, looks upward at the present battlements strangely deserted and inexplicably unprotected. *How desolate and lonely,* she thought. *Some tragedy happened here and now the castle abandoned.*

The turrets and towers reach dizzying heights. With panicked terror, she realizes the castle stood on the summit of a towering rocky precipice. *What a far, far drop to the rocks and water below,* her subconscious comments, with a nonchalance not corresponding to the rising tide of dread filling the reservoir of her heart and soul.

Then, she notices the highest tower. As she studies the bleak outline of the looming projection with uncharacteristic scientific detachment, startled to see it grow upward, rocketing into the sky like a sapling fed enchanted fertilizer. It matures in the blink of an eye, like the proverbial beanstalk sprung overnight to its full stature, born unbelievably from a handful of tiny magical beans. The shadow of the monstrosity dominates the rocky landscape, falls on her like the ominous shade of the moon during a solar eclipse. The exaggerated steeple, a mocking, nightmarish, and distorted reflection appears as an appendage on the castle's body. Her anticipation mounts as the tower sways and bows in perilous arcs like a top heavy and unsteady tree trunk in a gusty windstorm.

Suddenly, she realizes what happens. *There is a fall from the tower!* Her subconscious whispers. The words echo in her head with reverberating finality. *But who was the victim?* She questions. She looks frantically around her, searching the rocky terrain for a body or for any remnant evidence of the bloody impact. Seeing none, she turns back to face the castle, scanning the cliff side for a similar clue.

She hears some movement behind her. Turning, she sees a multitude of armor-clad soldiers suddenly surrounds her. Their warfare accoutrements are bright and colorful, in sharp contrast to the bleak backdrop of the castle. Swirls of olive green sweep over their battle shields like pounding ocean surf, embellished and broken by jagged and exaggerated lines of visceral lime and blood-red resembling shocking psychedelic lightning bolts. Steel helmets flash brightly with the blinding whiteness of reflecting sunlight and the colorful emblems on the sea of breastplates vaguely resemble the twisting union of two intertwined yellow serpents.

She frantically stumbles from one warrior to the other, inquiring about the recent tragedy on the tower. Receiving no response from any of the steel-encased mannequins, she accosts the nearest soldier, sending him crashing to the dusty ground with her forceful insistence.

"Who has fallen from the tower?" she screams. "Tell me now, Soldier! I need to know!"

Crouching by his side, she lifts his rusty visor. Aghast and startled, she staggers backwards, losing her balance, and falling onto the sharp bed of rocks behind her.

"No face - only air!" she gasps, horrified. The armor, a vacuous shell, encases an empty void and a vacuum of nothingness. The army of wraiths encircles and surrounds her. Trembling with fear, she closes her eyes, only to find her eyelids transparent. The empty faces everywhere, escape is impossible.

She holds her breath, prepares herself for asphyxiation at the hands of her phantom executioners, when suddenly, she no longer lies on the stone beach. *Has some omnipotent and unseen savior spirited me away from this army of ghostly murderers?* She asks perplexed by the abrupt change in scene.

Barefoot, she walks on the cold marble floor of a long and familiar corridor. A white cotton shirt clings loosely to her naked body, stirring almost imperceptibly on her skin from the gentle agitation of her swaying hips. Someone touches her right arm with soft reassurance and as she turns with trepidation to greet her mysterious and silent companion, her heart skips a beat.

"Rhys!" she beams, overjoyed to find her soul twin beside her. He wears no clothes, but a brilliant aura of white radiance surrounds him like a garment. "You are glorious!" she declares as he took her hand, leading her up a spiraling stairway ascending skyward.

The tower, she thinks with a mixture of elation and dread. *He is taking me to the tower!* She follows him without hesitation although she fears what they might find at the top.

One hundred and ninety-nine steps later, they reach a small room, scantly furnished but warmed by a small fire burning in a corner hearth. *This highest room is his as well as mine!* Her inner voice somehow knew. Turning to him, she takes his hands in hers as she laughs happily, gazing into his eyes.

"My room is yours," he confirms, as if he read her mind. "This," he demonstrates with a sweeping wave of his hand, "is my heart and my heart belongs to you, my dear sweet Gwen."

She embraces him, feeling his unspoiled whiteness envelope her like a womb. White like freshly fallen snow; white like the clouds on a clear spring day; white like sea foam riding on top of a crashing ocean wave; white like the true and untainted love she feels for him, her one and only partner, her lover for all eternity, and her betrothed in spirit. He was her soul twin.

He kisses her and all seems well, but only for a brief moment.

Wait! her subconscious cries. *There is more he does not tell!* Pulling away, she looks at his face. The lines of worry deep and heavy, the apprehension weighs like a stone on her fearful heart. "What is it, Rhys?" she asks, her voice tremulous.

"You are in danger here," he says, looking furtively around the empty room. "I fear for your safety."

"How so, Lover?" she inquires, her heart pounding in her chest.

He shakes his head, indicating he either did not know or else he refuses to say. She collapses at his feet, overcome with the heaviness she feels in her chest like a vise. "Tell me please," she begged. "Was I the one who fell from the tower?"

He does not answer. She grips his legs, weeping with frustration and angst. She must hear the answer. *Was it me?* The voice in her soul bellows. *He must tell me!*

"Rhys," she repeats into the silence, her voice chokes with fear and dread. Over and over again, she says his name, closing her eyes as she repeats her futile plea.

The scene changes, yet again. *What awaits me now?* She wonders. A strong wind blows her hair into wild disarray as it sings through the cracks and crevices of the battlements. The fabric of her chemise flaps against her body in the breeze like a sail battered by a gale force wind and she knows the flimsy garment cannot withstand the blustery onslaught much longer. In direct answer to this thought, a particularly strong gust of wind violently rips the blouse from her sensuous body.

I am outside! she realizes, opening her eyes to bravely face whatever strange twist of surrealism her dream offers her now. With shock, she finds herself on the tower balcony, naked and exposed, leaning out over the precarious drop with the delicious nudity of her quivering navel pushing vehemently against the cold stone of the railing. Her breasts dangle over the lip of the edge which touched the undersurface of her sexy globes like the groping hands of an excited lover.

She gasps with surprise and pleasure as she feels the welcome penetration of his cock behind her now, pushing her forcefully against the wall with each compelling and powerful thrust. Her eager orifice slippery and energized as his penis jackhammers, pounding her enthusiastic and agreeable pussy with the driving force of his exceptionally powerful sexual machine. He is deep inside her, but she wants more. Although his delectably brutal efforts quickly bring her to the peak of desire, her body screams for the violent climax to her heavenly torture.

"Harder," she hears her own screams, her emotions confused and contradictory, terrified, yet at the same time exhilarated. "Fuck my cunt, Rhys, hard and deep!"

His cock slams into her, crushing her body against the stone railing with every plunging thrust. Her orgasm will be painfully intense, she knows. She pants and moans, while his rigid ten-inch tool diligently works to complete the project between her legs. His penis splits her pussy like an axe ripping into soft wood and she screams with pleasure.

"Rhys," she cried, "I'm coming!" The stony tower of his masculinity, like a ramrod, shatters the wooden door of her castle's throne room. With the final insult, the door crashes open and releases the entire royal contents of her femininity like a thousand golden coins into the hallway of her pussy.

Her labia vises on to his cock as her climax spills over the edge of her consciousness to soak her dream-infused awareness. The sting of her burning release surges through her pubis cutting into her cervix and taking her breath away. The muscles of her groin and buttocks contract as if infused with tetanus, the spasms moving now to her cunt and anus.

She has his organ in a stranglehold and it twitches wildly as if it fights for its last breath. She feels the warm breath of his jism explode inside her, the last gasp of a defeated opponent. She cries out again, her triumph complete. "Oh, fuck yes!" she screams as the last quivering remnant of her climax dies in her loins.

Looking down, she notices her white cotton shirt apparently finds a temporary home on a narrow ledge five or six feet below the edge of the tower's rim. The ledge, perhaps three-feet wide, angles very slightly inward as it makes contact with the outer wall of the tower. It slopes gently downwards, following the circular contour of the outer parapet to disappear around the bend of its curving path. *A drainage ledge*, she somehow knows, *undoubtedly used to collect falling rainwater.* Given the castle's location on a rocky cliff, the castle's source of fresh drinking water, she knew came primarily from the bountiful skies.

Her dreamy focus returns to the blouse. *It must have fallen there, soon after it was ripped from my body by the relentless fingers of this breezy turbulence,* she reasons. The chemise flaps in the breeze; its animated movement seems almost human in the surrealistic script of her dream.

A lightheaded sensation overcomes her, a combination of sexual ecstasy and vertigo, she realizes. She looks down at the rocks far below, shuddering to think someone recently fell from this dizzying height.

She watches with curiosity, as her shirt flutters as the wind begins to pick up again. *Oh no,* she thinks with alarm, *it will fall!* She extends an arm in an attempt at recover, but before her hand reaches the fabric, it abruptly transforms into a majestic and beautiful osprey. The animal cocks its head, looks at Gwen with curiosity before diving off the ledge and in the blink of an eye. It spreads its six-foot wings and disappears.

At this moment, Rhys removes his cock from her pussy and she knows instantly she is doomed. His organ inside her, it seems, provided the connecting joist between their two bodies. Like a barbell suddenly snapping, the weight of her body falls away from his, sending her head first over the tower wall.

"Rhys!" she screams, hitting her shoulder as she lands forcefully on her side on the drainage ledge a few feet below. *Perhaps I am saved!* Hopefully, she thinks she can prevent the inevitable conclusion of her nightmare, but alas, the momentum of the six-foot drop causes her to roll.

His hand reaches out to save her, but it is too late. "Rhys," she calls, over and over again, as she plummets towards her rocky graveyard.

What will it feel like to die? she wonders with detached interest, somehow feeling as if she an observer rather than the victim. She tumbles through the air, the landscape fast approaching in a jumbled chaotic blur making her head swim with nausea.

"Rhys, help me!" she calls a final time as the ground rushes up to greet her.

She braces for the impact. "Goodbye, my love," she whispers, cringing and covering her head as if these gestures will soften the impending collision.

She hears him call her name, echoing with agonized despair from the top of the tower. His sweet and calming voice, so far away, so lonely, so desperate... and oh so compelling! She wills herself to heed his call and as if by magic, she awoke with a start, lying by his side in his warm and comfortable bed.

She was safe and he was, in fact, calling her name!

***

"Gwen!" he said. "Wake up, sweet one!"

It took a moment for her to orient. Peering around, she saw Rhys, at the side of the bed, calling her name as he dressed hurriedly.

She heard urgent rapping at the door which Rhys evidently prepared to answer. If they discovered her like this, naked in his bed and flushed from their recent lovemaking, they would both pay a deadly price!

She leapt out of bed, covered herself with a small white coverlet from a tossed chair in the corner. She stepped behind an armoire, large enough to effectively conceal her. Rhys, in the meantime, walked cautiously to the door, opened it a crack to converse with the caller on the other side.

"What is it, Bridie?" she heard him ask.

The high-pitched reply shook her to her very core. "It's Niamh!" she heard the midwife say. "She is gone, m'Lord!"

A moment of silence, as Rhys tried to process this shocking news. Finally, he spoke. "Gone, Woman?" he asked. "How could that be?"

"She was in her cradle when we last checked," she replied nervously. "Young Deidra fell asleep in the chair at the baby's side and when she awoke, the child had disappeared!"

Suddenly, Gwen knew. *The tower!* she thought with panic and dread. *Mahrea has taken Niamh to the tower!*

Gwen rushed from her hiding place, unconcerned about her continued concealment. "The tower, Rhys!" she cried. "The baby has been taken to the tower!"

She rushed passed him, threw the door open and pushed Bridie aside as she ran frantically into the corridor.

"I must save her!" she yelled over her shoulder as she hurried down the hallway, her naked body barely concealed by the scant covering she hugged to her chest as she ran.

As she heard Rhys' footsteps following closely behind her, she prayed to God they were not too late.

Chapter Nine
The Tower

Rhys struggled to comprehend what happened as he watched without reacting at first as Gwen rushed passed him in a flash of white skin and fabric. As if in slow motion, he saw her sprint down the hall in her bare feet, her scant covering fluttered behind her in the breeze created by her panicked and hasty flight towards the tower stairway. The ornamental tassels on the coverlet rippled chaotically against her bare skin as she raced quickly towards her destination and swayed like branches in a wind-swept forest. Her soft pale nudity flashed like dappled patches of filtered sunlight.

It took him a moment to respond, but in a split second, he dashed after her down the dimly lit corridor. Like lovesick Apollo, in hot pursuit of his beloved but elusive Daphne, he closed the gap between them with quick and lanky strides. Her nymph's hair trailed and flowed behind her like the leafy laurel branches of her mythical counterpart as she ran. He smelt the intoxicating aroma of her wind-swept locks as he overtook her at the base of the tower stairs.

He stopped her with a hand on her shoulder, spun her around gently before she began her frantic ascent up the winding and seemingly endless staircase. With a start, he saw a wild but honest panic in her eyes warn him not to tarry too long in his inquiries.

"Explain, Lover!" he demanded between heavy breaths.

"We have very little time!" she panted. She looked anxiously up the stairwell, attempting without success to free herself from the strong grip of his hands on her shoulders. She stared pleadingly into his eyes. "For God's sake, release me Rhys!" she cried. "We may be too late to save her!"

"What has happened?" he asked. "I do not understand."

"She has taken Niamh to the top!" Gwen explained, her words tumbling over each other with awkward haste. "We must stop her, Rhys. There is murder in her heart!"

His mind reeled. "Who, Gwen?" And in a flash, he understood. "Mahrea!" he exclaimed.

"Yes!" she panted. "I have seen the evil in her eyes, Rhys!" She paused, her face unmistakably gripped with worry and fear. "And I have seen images of what may come to pass if we do not intervene," she confided, her voice faltered with emotion.

"Images?" he asked, trying to comprehend her fragmented train of thought.

"In my dream!" she explained. "We must hurry, Rhys, before Niamh falls to her death at the witch's hands!"

The word jolted him. "Witch," he murmured. Gwen's acknowledgment of his own suspicions solidified his resolve. He released her abruptly and dashed past her onto the stairs behind. Taking three steps at a time, he felt the urgency of the moment as he pushed himself to the limit in a marathon sprint to the tower's summit.

He sensed as if he careened wildly towards some unknown destination, saddled precariously on the unpredictable and untamed stallion of destiny. Each stair, each landing, and each stone of the tower's well flashed by him in a confused rush much like the jumbled images from the past three days, three months, and three years that swirled in his bewildered brain. *Will I ever arrive at the end of this hair-raising journey?* he questioned. If so, he needed Gwen's help to piece together the blurred fragments of his experience and make his incoherent existence meaningful again.

He easily outpaced her. In fact, he barely heard her echoing footsteps following below and far behind him. The sound of her trailing pursuit appeared like the memory of their undying and ancient love for each other - distant but never forgotten, far away but fast approaching, ethereal yet palpable, constant and unfading.

His legs ached with the strenuous effort of his haste. How many stairs had he climbed, and how many still left to go? *Surely I have covered at least half the distance by now!* he thought. A hundred steps behind and just under a hundred yet ahead. His heart pounded with tense anxiety and physical exertion as he rushed onward, hoping beyond hope that he could save his precious daughter before the unthinkable happened. *Whatever waits at the top,* he thought, *I will face alone.* He would risk death itself to save his daughter and protect his sweet Gwen.

He started to sweat despite the cold. Blinking to clear his vision, he noticed the final landing now through eyes blurred by the moisture of his perspiration and altered by the rush of his accelerated circulation. The destination platform was indistinct in the confining darkness of the windowless stone silo. He squinted as he noticed a faint shaft of brightness which extended like a gangplank from the edge of the landing. *Sunlight*, he realized, *cutting like a sword into the dense atmosphere of the spiraling staircase.* The first light of morning reached its hopeful arm through the partially opened doorway, beckoning him with its soft and convincing entreaty to enter, if he dared.

I will face my nemesis and meet my destiny with courage and resolve! he pledged as he leapt onto the solid and bulky stone platform. Without hesitation, he pushed open the door, rushing without thought into the tower room, primed and prepared to act immediately on his daughter's behalf, regardless of the circumstance or danger.

The sunrise, a burning orange ball, hovered on the horizon to cast its blinding glare over the balcony railing directly into his line of vision. Unprepared for the blazing offensive, he could not react quickly enough to neutralize the ambush. His vision, bleached temporarily a brilliant white, rendered helpless by the scorching onslaught of the morning sun. He held out his hand to block the radiance while his overwhelmed rods and cones struggled to recharge.

He cursed the impatience that prompted his thoughtless and headlong rush into the lion's den, which resulted in this potentially fatally setback. As his vision slowly recovered, the shadow of his wife-turned-adversary came into blurry focus. She stood at the doorway leading to the balcony; the sunlight behind her formed a sinister halo around the dark outline of her silhouette. He could not see her face, but had no difficulty recognizing the gleaming object she held in front of her in her outstretched palms.

The orb, a miniature sun, glowed like a tiny inferno in the cradle made by its mistress's hands. Streams of combustion-like energy jumped from the crystal-like solar sunspots. In fact, the globe seemed to harbor an impending conflagration. Rhys, expected the ball to burst into flames at any moment, was surprised Mahrea could clutch the object without suffering third degree burns.

"I have been expecting you, my foolhardy husband," she said quietly.

"Where is Niamh?" he demanded, taking three steps forward.

She extended her arms and the orb burned brighter. He felt as if a two-ton weight dropped upon his shoulders. *I cannot move!* he realized with horror as a heavy weariness descended upon him. He willed his aching and burning limbs to respond to his mental command for action, but they answered now to another master.

"You are helpless, my dear Thane," she sneered. "The power of my orb is limitless, husband. Your body is now mine to command, due to my crystal's magic."

He found he could still talk. "The baby, Mahrea!" he croaked. His voice choked on his dry and parched throat. "Where is my child?" he managed to ask, his words a hoarse whisper.

"You are too late," she shrugged. "The poor helpless infant is balanced on the brink of the precipice, Husband. In a moment, she will roll off and no one but you will grieve when she passes from this world to the next."

Her chilling words rang in his ears with the finality of a death sentence pronounced on the innocent defendant by a cruel and heartless judge. She was a ghost-like specter in his fading vision, no longer on the balcony, but approaching him now as the room began to spin.

On his knees, he struggled to breath, to fight, to live. *I am indeed helpless!* he realized. Mahrea rendered him incapacitated, in the blink of an eye, by her insidious magic, against which there was no possible contest. As he lost consciousness, he felt her breath in his ear and her voice in his head.

"Do not struggle, Husband, there is truly no point," she cooed as she stroked his hair. "You will not die, I assure you. I need you alive."

He questioned her with his eyes, her face a rapidly fading shadow. "Yes, Husband... you must live. I will need your potent seed again, soon, to fertilize my womb and sire my warlock son."

An empty blackness engulfed him as her last words drifted through his psyche. "A son you will yet give me, of this I am sure!"

***

Mahrea gazed with satisfaction at her defeated prey. Her unconscious husband laid prone beside her, his respirations shallow and his lips a pale, dusky grey. *What an effortless victory*, she scoffed.

"Make sure he lives," she commanded aloud, addressing the nebulous orb she clasped tightly in her hands. As if in response, the churning cloud of energy instantly changed colors, pulsing in dark blue subservience to its evil mistress who rose from her crouching position to stand triumphantly over her victim.

She laughed to herself. The great warlord lay defenseless on the cold stone floor, paralyzed and oblivious like a jellyfish stranded on a hopeless expanse of deserted and lonely beach. *He is powerless now,* she thought. *Now my plan will proceed on schedule and without his meddling and annoying interference!* she gloated, feeling drunk with the elation of her victory.

She looked over her shoulder; her eyes squinted to see past the glare of the rising sun. *Is that the child, still balanced on the stone balcony railing?* she asked with disbelief. She was truly startled to see the child still lived.

She placed the tiny infant on her back, expecting she would topple off the edge of the railing almost immediately. The blustery gusts of the strong February wind pushed and pulled the baby's lightweight body like the compelling digits of Hel, the Norse goddess of death. Niamh's tiny limbs, flayed helplessly in the air, instinctively countered the invisible assault from Hell's windy offensive. An insignificant boat wandering innocently into an ocean tempest, her body swayed perilously back and forth on the brink of the ledge. Her weak and high-pitched cries barely heard over the howl of the frigid winter blast. Her fragile body, loosely wrapped in a thin infant's mantle, shivered in an unsuccessful attempt to warm itself. *She will surely die of exposure if she does not fall to her death soon,* Mahrea reassured herself, as she watched with macabre curiosity at the struggling infant.

She will not die by my hand, Mahrea rationalized as she pondered the baby's fate. The infant would either die naturally by exposure to the elements or she would fall to her death inadvertently. *Either way, I hold no culpability in this affair,* she reasoned, satisfied this perverted logic purged her of any and all responsibility in her daughter's untimely and tragic demise. Like Pontius Pilate, she would not be held accountable for the impending execution she facilitated.

As Lady Macbeth did after Duncan's murder, she studied her hands with detached interest, but unlike the literary villainess, Mahrea had no conscience. *They are clean,* she concluded, feeling no guilt for her heinous crime against her own blood, for in her chest resided a cold and compassionless heart.

She walked happily towards the balcony door, reviewing in her mind the next step in her revenge plans. So far, her right-on-target presumptions, allowed her carefully planned strategy to be executed with the flawless and deadly precision of a sharpshooter's arrow. She knew the nursery servants would immediately alert her husband once they discovered the empty crib and as she hoped, the first stop in Rhys's frantic search for his daughter would be his tower sanctuary. *What a shame he did not witness the child's death,* she lamented. The trauma of such an experience might have permanently broken his will, she mused, making him a pliable and malleable lump of inert and lifeless clay in her manipulative sculptress's hands.

No matter, she shrugged, responding by gesture to the animated conversation that chattered in her mind. *I will make certain he witnesses his lover's deadly fall from the tower's peak,* she pledged silently. *It will scar him for life, of this I am certain!*

She spoke out loud, having reached her decision. "Globe," she boomed, "you will summon the girl and when she arrives, you will release the Thane from his unnaturally induced sleep, just in time to see his defeated lover on her knees, begging me for mercy."

Who is this girl, and where is she at this very moment? she wondered. With a burning fury in her chest, she recalled the provocative and disturbing images the globe shown her hours before. "The sultry bitch will pay," she promised, remembering the look of ecstasy on the girl's face as she enjoyed Rhys large cock penetrating her pussy from behind.

She had been in his bedroom, this much was clear. *How in the world had she gained access to the castle and to the Thane's private bedchamber without arousing suspicion?* she asked herself. *Could she be a servant in this very castle, perhaps?* she sneered, dismissing this unlikely possibility.

"The girl is probably a whore," she commented, pleased with this alternative explanation. She smiled, imagining the pitiful desperation involved in such an encounter. "The poor deprived thane," she sneered sarcastically, laughing at the thought of her husband fucking a common prostitute and all because she denied him the privilege of her sexual favors!

Her mood switched, as her amusement replaced by a burning jealousy. *If the wench was paid to spread her legs,* she thought, *she will, in turn, pay dearly for this insolence with her own life! She will never fuck my husband again,* she vowed. Homicide seethed in her veins like scalding red-hot magma immediately prior to a devastating volcanic eruption.

The orb was a deep sanguine red; its swirling contents resembled an agitated pool of oozing blood. She closed her eyes, focused on psychic integration with her mental appendage. *Call her now!* she commanded, wondering if the girl already left the castle.

Come to the tower! Mahrea urged her voice and the globe's. They chanted in harmony, an alarm call only the girl could hear. *Make haste, dear lady, come now! Your lover is dying!* Anxious now to complete her evil task, she hoped the harlot was close by.

Little did she know how close, since, at that very moment, Rhys's mistress was only a few short yards away, on the other side of the landing door.

***

Gwen stood on the landing, catching her breath for a moment after her frantic dash to the top of the stairs. Rhys, more accustomed to physical exertion, easily won the race, arriving a full three or four minutes before her. *I must join him to face our mutual enemy,* she thought between breaths as she started towards the partially opened door.

She stopped. A voice whispered in her brain and the message was urgent. *Make haste,* it said, coaxing and pleading her to embark on a journey she completed.

In an instant, she had dual revelations. Not only did she realize the voice in her head was Mahrea's, but she also understood that incredibly and fortuitously, the witch had no knowledge whatsoever of Gwen's imminent arrival!

She thinks I am elsewhere! she reasoned, feeling hopeful she might use the element of surprise to her advantage. *This is my one chance to overpower her with an abrupt and unexpected entrance!*

She quietly prepared herself for a mad rush into the fray. Taking a deep breath and drawing upon every ounce of her emotional and physical strength, she threw herself forcefully against the wooden door, rushing headlong into the chamber like an enraged and incited she-wolf, intent on her mission of rescue and retaliation.

Screaming at the top of her lungs like an Amazon warrior maiden, she hoped to crush and overwhelm her formidable opponent with the force of her righteous determination. She barreled into Mahrea, who, being engaged in the demanding and oblivious preoccupation of her telepathic trance, was unprepared for the unexpected assault which came from nowhere.

They tumbled together onto the cold stone floor, rolling like one chaotic entity through the balcony doorway and onto the mile-high terrace. Gwen, whose intuition told her much of Mahrea's power derived from the burning maroon crystal she held in her hands, prayed the impact of her tackle disengaged the globe from its owner. She breathed a sigh of relief as Mahrea clutched at Gwen with both of her empty hands. Looking back into the tower room, Gwen's hopes for this small but important victory confirmed. With elation, she saw the glimmering orphaned sphere of energy, propelled by the momentum of Gwen's assault, resting with quiet discontent near Rhys's motionless body.

She only caught a fleeting glimpse of her lover, but what she saw chilled her to the bone. The tragic significance of his immobility took a moment to hit home. "Rhys!" she cried with alarm and despair. *How will I be able to live, if he is gone?* she asked herself, as she by necessity forced herself to return her concentration to the life and death struggle with her lover's killer in progress.

She is responsible, her inner voice screamed with justified rage as she encircled Mahrea's throat with both hands. "What have you done to him?" she demanded, her voice hardly audible over the forlorn and lamenting cry of the frigid February wind.

The coverlet draped loosely and precariously over her shoulders, flapped wildly in the gusty breeze. Her hands occupied and she unable to prevent the inevitable loss of her makeshift garment. Like a majestic eagle, the blanket lifted itself into the air, hovering for a moment in suspended indecision before it flew avian-like, to rest for a moment on the stone railing to the right. Like Gwen, who shivered in her naked and vulnerable exposure, the piece of fabric found itself at the mercy of the elements. Its feeble attempts to resist the forceful winter blast futile and with a fluttering wave goodbye, the white wings of her one-time impromptu chemise disappeared over the balcony edge.

In a flash, the eerie parallels to her dream became apparent. Here she was, naked on the tower, stripped of her covering by the identical windy mechanism her dream described. And, at this very moment, she was quite certain the blanket rested on the exterior tower ledge, mimicking its psychic fabricated counterpart in every imaginable detail of this surrealistic reality.

As she tightened her grip on Mahrea's throat, she noticed movement on the railing, off to the left and directly opposite from where her coverlet disappeared. Her heart pounded with horror and disbelief. *What kind of monster would place a child in such jeopardy, let alone her very own flesh and blood?* she wondered as a sickening nausea churned in her stomach. With horror, she watched as the helpless infant teetered back and forth on the railing, harassed by the same gusty wind that had just sent Gwen's blanket over the brink. Like a novice tightrope walker who would soon succumb to gravity's inevitable pull, the baby struggled to resist the forceful tug and push of the wintry gale. If a savior did not intervene soon, the child would fall off the edge and plunge onto the rocky beach below.

Gwen knew what to do. Without hesitation, she released her hold on the witch's neck, rushing to prevent a disaster on its way to a dreadful conclusion. She watched with mounting panic as the baby started to roll over the edge. *This is a race I cannot win,* she realized with sinking despair as she reached the stone railing.

Niamh disappeared, her fate sealed a mere split second before Gwen successfully intervened. "No," she cried aloud, refusing to accept the baby's terminal fate so easily. *You must save the baby, no matter what the cost!* her motherly instinct commanded.

She simply could not ignore the call of her maternal inner voice. Without thinking, she leapt over the railing without breaking her stride - her hands, arms and shoulders providing the lever and fulcrum upon which her pivoting body swung smoothly and without effort from the safety of the balcony to the dangerous and empty altitude beyond. Like an Olympic pole-vaulter, she found she cleared the edge with effortless ease and was at gravity's mercy on the far side of her jumper's arc.

In a moment I will fall to my death, she realized with odd detachment as if she were observed someone else's predicament rather than her own. *And no one in this world or the next will be able to save me.*

***

Rhys awoke in a confused daze. He laid face down on the cold stone floor, his cheek pressed to the hard grey granite, the enforced intimacy of this harsh contact reminding him of his empty and loveless marital relationship. His head swam with the dizzying remnant of near asphyxiation well on its way to becoming a pounding headache. The restraints of her binding spell clearly loosened, since his numb limbs now moved easily. He slowly and cautiously pushed himself off the floor and onto his hands and knees, satisfied he would soon be able to support his full weight on his rapidly recovering legs.

As he shook the fog from his recovering brain, his eyes focused on the three or four feet of granite scenery in his immediate field of vision. He blinked, unwilling at first to believe his eyes. He must either be dreaming or hallucinating. *This cannot be!* he thought with stunned but hopeful disbelief.

Mahrea's deadly energy globe rested with quiet enticement a mere six inches from his right hand as if it rolled there intentionally and of its own accord. Like a double agent whose true allegiance revealed, the orb pulsed with soft blue seduction, begging for immediate de-briefing with a new owner and a fresh alliance.

He would not be able to channel the crystal's powerful energy, of this he knew, but having it in his possession might neutralize or eliminate Mahrea's potent and evil magic. He reached for the orb as he formed his strategy and rose to his feet at the same moment his hand touched the globe.

The soothing blue appearance of the witch's tool was a cruel and misleading deception. The traitorous entity sizzled in his hand like a smoking ball of dry ice. Despite the excruciating pain, which cut like a saber from his hand to his shoulder, he clutched the orb with gritty determination. *I cannot possess this demon for long,* he concluded *but I must somehow destroy it, before it destroys me!*

He staggered forward, reached the door to the balcony with no insignificant effort. He took in the scene like a battle survivor scanning the field for signs of his enemy. His entire arm throbbed as the evil humors from the swirling orb penetrated each and every pore of his being, like a deadly poison that eagerly soaked into his very core. *I will not last long at this rate,* he realized with mounting pessimism as the pain in his arm gripped him like the jaws of a manticore.

The sun was like a magician's prop, levitated by invisible hands to a higher position on the horizon's stage during the brief interlude of Rhys's semi-coma. Nature's slight-of-hand performance removed the sun's glare from the backdrop of the balcony arena, allowing him an unhindered view of the evolving scene. Rhys scanned the platform and the deserted stone railings, with a sinking heart.

"My sweet Niamh," he cried the profound despair audible in his cracking voice. He dropped to his knees, overwhelmed by the combination of heart-breaking loss and unbearable physical pain.

Mahrea rose to her feet. Although her expression portrayed a smug confidence, Rhys thought he detected a hint of concern beneath her steely facade. Her fixed on the globe he clutched in his shaking hand betrayed the importance of her sphere to the outcome of their escalating conflict.

"You have lost, Husband," she said, giving the impression she considered her victory a foregone conclusion, despite his possession of her psychic appendage.

He mustered every ounce of his strength, rising to his feet to face his opponent for their final confrontation. "I have your globe, inhuman sorceress!" he announced, his voice strong and confidant. He raised the orb like a weapon, banking on his assumption she needed it to focus and direct her supernatural energy.

"It matters not," she shrugged, feigned indifference. "I have already won, you fool. I no longer need the crystal!"

Her lips quivered slightly, betraying her true reliance on the orb as the source of her evil power. Her eyes fixed on his hand, her expression thoughtful. *She is weighing her options*, he concluded, *and I must act fast. If she rushes me, she might in fact overpower me, given my weakened state.*

"You lie, Witch!" he boomed, actually surprising himself with the strength and conviction he projected in his voice. "You need this tool. Without it, you are an empty and powerless shell."

Her face dropped slightly, informing him he indeed spoke the truth. Quickly recovering her composure, she took a step forward.

"Stop," he ordered. He raised the globe in a gesture suggesting no misinterpretation. "I will throw it and it will be lost forever!"

His threat had its desired effect. She stopped, frozen by a misdirected spell that had somehow backfired. She held up both hands, palms out, in grudging conciliation.

Her voice softened. "I love you, Rhys," she cooed, her voice coated with unconvincing sweetness. "You and I can start again, now that the barriers to our success and happiness have been removed." Her words, an injection of bitter reality, jolted him to an enhanced understanding of the tragic repercussions of her manipulations. *Barriers,* he repeated to himself. The plural word choice pointed to an unavoidable conclusion.

"Gwen!" he cried. "Where is she, Witch?"

Her face hardened as she recognized the ineffectiveness of her fresh tactic. She smiled the macabre satisfaction evident in her leering countenance.

"Ah, Gwen," she mused, her words steeped in sarcasm. "If I had only known her name, I might have called out a warning. It seems she was unaware of the steep drop on the far side of the railing." She sniggered, amused by the cruel irony in her morbid observation.

"Murderer," he managed to whisper, choking on his tears of regret and sadness. "You murdered them both!"

She shrugged, unaffected by his accusation. He felt nauseated by her unbelievable nonchalance. "Infanticide and murder," he hissed, overwhelmed by loathing and disgust for the inhuman monster facing him on the tower balcony.

She shook her head. "Neither, Husband. The child was taken by your very own kind and loving God," she sneered. "You see, she rolled off on her own accord, with no assistance from any worldly being." She walked towards the railing, ran her fingers along the stone as if she caressed a lover.

Turning to face him again, she continued. "And your whore acted quite impulsively," she explained. "She simply jumped," she said, an expression of mock concern on her face. She shrugged again. "I suppose she stupidly hoped to save the child, somehow."

She paused, searching Rhys's face for some reaction. Her persistent verbal cruelty burned like dry tinder on a bed of hot coals. Her arrogant and insensitive boastfulness stoked his fury, soon to burst into a fiery and vengeful conflagration.

She seemed unaware of - or unconcerned about - the mounting rage in his warrior's heart. She continued her abusive ranting. "What a brave and fearless harlot," she said, shaking her head sarcastically and clucking her tongue for extra emphasis. "The sweet thing sacrificed herself needlessly. In the end, she was nothing but a laughable fool and an idealistic idiot."

He heard enough. The years of frustration, combined with the futile and senseless loss of all important and dear to him, exploded like gas under pressure in the core of his very being. He felt the strength of all his goodness and purity surge into his right arm, instantly neutralizing the pain and hatred that emanated from the pulsing orb. With an awesome inner strength far exceeding any force or energy he previously known, he drew his arm back, preparing for the ultimate test of his bravery and integrity.

"You will be judged, not by me, but by a higher power!" he cried. "I intend to leave you untouched, demon, but your orb I will destroy!"

A look of panic gripped her face with the abruptness of a stranglehold. His intention clear and judging from her expression, she was fully cognizant of his resolute objective. He would rocket the crystal into the oblivion of the distant ocean and in so doing effectively sever the umbilical cord linking globe and mistress. This way, the orb lay powerless, resting harmlessly on the sandy carpet of Poseidon's deepest throne room.

Cocking his arm back, his powerful muscles tensed like a loaded slingshot, tendons stretched to the breaking point in anxious preparation for the imminent release of the deadly projectile. The catapult primed and a split second later, the safety peg kicked clear. His arm shot forward like the rippling limb of a mighty discus thrower, propelling the orb in a blur of speed and unstoppable momentum.

As the sphere left his hand, so did the pain, so abruptly it felt as if he gripped a live electric eel. His aim high, impelling the globe on a trajectory easily clearing the railing with yards to spare. *The deed is done,* he thought with confidence, never dreaming Mahrea would ever be able to intercept the speeding missile.

The next five seconds transpired in a flash, but played out his disbelieving mind in slow motion would change his life forever. Mahrea reached for the soaring crystal with outstretched arms as if the gesture would redirect the wayward projectile and alter its course. Eyes closed in concentration, her lips moved as if she recited some unnatural incantation. In direct response, it seemed the orb, arced in a downward path, headed directly for its owner like a heat-seeking weapon. With horror and dismay, Rhys realized Mahrea's summons most likely succeeded.

But wait! The globe careened towards its mistress at such a lightning speed it certainly would lead to a most destructive impact if the satellite continued on its present course. *Perhaps the fleeting but sustained contact with foreign flesh confused the orb's identity!* Rhys postulated, his hope increased with each passing millisecond as the globe continued its kamikaze suicide dive towards its unsuspecting target.

Mahrea seemed oblivious to the impending collision. Eyes closed, she continued to recite her retrieval spell, expecting to reclaim a passive and compliant dove rather than an aggressive and resentful hawk. The crystal, now a fiery red meteor, hurled through the air with whistling precision. Anticipating the impact, Rhys threw himself face down on the balcony stone. Covering his head with his arms, he watched as the witch's boomerang returned to its rightful owner.

She opened her eyes just in time to recognize the danger. She ducked, avoiding direct contact, but unable to avert inevitable disaster. The vehicle of destruction crashed like a comet into the stone railing directly behind her. Curiously, it disappeared without a trace and without a sound as it was absorbed and incorporated into the balcony stone like a ghostly hologram. Much like the out of sync pause between a flash of lightning and its delayed thundering consequence, Rhys sensed the horrific implication of the orb's impact would take a moment to flourish. He braced for the inevitable, as he waited for the falling blade of the guillotine to perform its obligatory task.

Sure enough, the segment of railing sustaining the impact glowed a fiery red before imploding with a deafening and shattering crash. The stone literally disappeared into nothingness as if magically transformed from solid to gas by the infective integration of the orb's atomic energy. The six-foot gaping hole a powerful but short-lived vortex sucked the air from the balcony into the emptiness of the surrounding altitude.

The awesome force exerted its brief but inescapable sovereignty like a tyrannical despot. Mahrea, unprepared for the dramatic negative surge of energy, pulled backwards and outward through the defect in the balcony railing and into the empty air beyond. With a scream, she disappeared from view, arms flailed as she unsuccessfully attempted to renegotiate her inexorable and justified fate.

Rhys found himself pressed against an intact segment of railing, immediately adjacent to the orb's gaping handiwork. The implosion pulled him forcefully across the balcony floor so rapidly he did not realize until after the fact he had been relocated by the globe's confused expression of destructive energy.

All was quiet now. Mahrea plummeted to her death, suffering the same fate she inflicted on innocent Niamh and dear sweet Gwen. He felt a confused mixture of emotions: relief and thankfulness he won his own battle, anger and self-reproach that he had failed so miserably in his role as savior and protector and profound sorrow over the senseless loss of child and lover. He struggled to comprehend the futility of such a pointless tragedy as he picked himself off the granite platform, readying himself for his final personal challenge in this appalling and sickening ordeal.

I must confirm that she is dead. He worried she may invoke the sorcery to escape gravity's crushing and heavy hand. *She is a witch,* he reminded himself as he gripped the cold stone railing with trembling and cautious hands. *Expect the unexpected, Rhys!* his inner voice warned as he peered fearfully over the edge.

With relief, he saw the dark outline of her lifeless body far below, sprawled on the rocks like a discarded and tattered rag doll, lying face down in an expanding maroon pool of blood. He breathed a sigh of relief, watching as a wave rolled softly over the corpse in a futile attempt to awaken the sleeper. *She will not rise.* He silently informed the ocean's figurative hand. *She will rest in hell now, for all eternity.*

He closed his eyes, dreading the visual search for his baby and his mistress. Steeling his nerves, he opened his eyes, moist with the tears of grief and regret. Scanning the rocky beach, he looked carefully for signs of the witch's two innocent victims. Seeing nothing, he furrowed his brow, baffled, and perplexed by the emptiness of the beach below.

Perhaps they have been carried away already by the waves, he thought. *Or their bodies drifted as they dropped, pushed by a strong gust of wind during their fall, to land on a piece of beach far to the left or to the right of the expected location.* He leaned over, this second postulate seeming much more likely than the first. He carefully scanned the far reaches of the beach to the right, but saw nothing.

Looking to the left, he gasped with shock and surprise. He knew immediately what he saw with his stunned and disbelieving eyes would be indelibly and forever imprinted on his deepest heart and soul.

***

Gwen realized she must act fast if she wished to avert a fatal disaster. She trusted the vision in her dream without questioning its validity, relying on the accuracy of her nightmare, which shown her an exterior ledge on the far side of the tower's edge.

As she threw her legs over the battlement with the ease of a gymnast, she repositioned her hands, gripped the inner edge of the railing with desperate and tenuous fingers. Her arms broke the momentum of her swinging body with a jolt, causing her to ricochet inward as the direction of her body's velocity became redirected with abrupt and reciprocal intensity. Her torso slammed against the exterior wall, her nakedness slid and bounced against the gritty stone, which scratched and bruised her pristine and perfect skin with sadistic, abrasive proficiency.

She gasped. The crippling pain in her hands and knuckles clearly exceeded the ache in her shoulders and the burning sting of her bleeding nipples. Her fingers struggled, unable to support her weight for more than a few additional seconds. Looking down, she saw her dream spoke true. The exterior ledge was a reality, not a fantasy and within easy reach, a mere two feet below her dangling feet!

"Thank God in heaven," she whispered thankfully. She released her hold on the stone railing, dropped gratefully and safely onto the narrow stone shelf below.

She had been spared the long drop to the rocks below. The wind blew forcefully against her, threatening to push her off balance and send her plunging to her death. She pressed her naked body against the cold stone, searching the flat granite with her hands for a defect into which she might insert her aching fingers. She found a weathered crack between two stone blocks, which nature widened just enough to accommodate two of her slim digits. *Better than nothing,* she thought as she clung desperately to the frozen rock wall.

What has become of Niamh? she wondered fearfully. She looked cautiously to her left, finding no sign of the infant on the upwardly sloping segment of the slender sill. Facing the wall again, she waited for a strong gust of wind to pass before looking apprehensively to the right.

Oh my God! she whispered joyfully, as she gazed on a miraculous sight indeed. The helpless infant fell, by God's grace, directly into a large osprey nest, fortuitously situated on the drainage ledge directly beneath the child's precarious position on the tower's railing. Niamh rested comfortably on her back, uninjured and safe in her avian cradle, thanks to the expertly woven crib of grass, twigs, and branches meticulously fashioned by very same bird of prey nervously perched on the down-sloping tower outcropping, a mere three feet away.

Gwen inched her way towards her surrogate daughter. Despite the nest's generous upturned rim, Gwen still worried the infant might inadvertently roll over the lip of the makeshift bed and fall to a tragic and premature death. The osprey watched with curiosity as the baby's protector made very slow headway on her precarious journey. Six feet seemed like six miles, as the wind whipped forcefully around her, a deliberate and mocking deterrent to a successful rescue. *Slowly*, she told herself, as she finally and arduously reached her destination.

The osprey watched Gwen's slow progress with curiosity. She tilted her head, perhaps to acknowledge the official changing of the guard. A moment later, her shift concluded and her commission relieved, she was gone, spreading her six-foot wings as she navigated the windy current in majestic flight.

She is the bird from my dream! Gwen realized suddenly, crouching next to the nest with her right hand on Niamh's chest to insure the baby's safety while the fingers of her left hand found happy and solid purchase on the rim of nature's bed of salvation. "Thank you, dear friend, for watching over my sweet child," she whispered thankfully to the soaring plumed savior, whose outline was no more than a pinpoint speck on the horizon.

She heard voices on the balcony, but the words lost in the cry of the howling winter wind. *Is it Rhys?* she wondered hopefully, straining without success to hear above the screaming current swirled around her and the roaring waves crashed far below. *Oh, dear God,* she prayed, *let it be Rhys and protect him from her evil vengeance!*

In direct answer to her supplication, it seemed, she suddenly rocked by a shock wave as the adjacent stone railing seemed to disintegrate into thin air, a mere six feet from where she knelt on the tower's shelf-like precipice. Simultaneously, a body rocketed past her, propelled through the air.

She knew immediately it was Mahrea. Her brilliant red hair, flamed in wild disarray around her beautiful face, burned like the very fire of Hades as she fell. The sorceress struggled with futile desperation, her arms flailed against empty air, as she dropped to the rocks below.

Gwen closed her eyes. Although the witch's death well-deserved, she simply could not bear to watch the final impact. She waited a moment, until she no longer heard the sound of Mahrea's quickly fading screams.

She opened her eyes. "It is over," she declared gratefully, peering over the edge to view the lifeless corpse below.

The evidence their ordeal was truly over, lay motionless face down on her rocky deathbed. Gwen shuddered. *That could have easily been me,* she thought. "Thank you," she whispered, eyeing the heavens with grateful appreciation.

And then she saw him: palpable and real, pure and good, kind and worthy, and so astoundingly alive! The moment was a treasured portrait she would lock in her sacred chest of memories for all time.

"My love," she whispered quietly, knowing full well that he could not hear her. "Look this way, darling... I am here!"

He looked to his right and then to his left. Their eyes met and the world stopped.

And she knew, without a doubt, her new life only just begun.

Epilogue

And so ends our tale, dear reader: about a husband, wife, mistress, Thane, witch, nursemaid, hero, demon, angel, a man, his onerous duty, and his one true love.

And so begins another tale, faithful audience: about a father, a mother, their children, a Thane, his lady, and their family: the Lord of Dunscaith, the Mistress of Skye, and their happy progeny.

I hear the clamor rising from these pages, but I must hold firm. The story of the Thane and Mistress of Skye is a tale that simply must wait, Patient Audience. There is much to tell, dear reader, enough to fill another volume and maybe more. Strife and harmony, peace and war, love and hate, discontent and satisfaction - all of these things will be told, but in the due course of time. For now, you must content yourselves with my assurance. Their love for each other is true and pure; the bond between them grows ever stronger with each passing day and long and passionate night.

But hark! Your arguments ring in my ears, cause me to stray from my firm resolve. Prithee, hold your protests, clamoring crowd, I am a reasonable and conscientious bard. I have heard your complaints and I offer you now a gentle compromise. I will leave you with a morsel, which I hope, will feed your craving for a happy conclusion and quench your thirst for a very unlikely but thoroughly satisfying coincidence.

Let us fast forward to a day in the early spring, ten years after the harrowing scene on the balcony tower. After the witch's demise, Rhys took the beautiful Gwenhwyvar as his wife and lady and never before or after, had there been or would there be, a more perfect union between a man and a woman. Gwen's son, whom she named Dugal, in memory of Rhys' peasant alias, joined his new family at Dunscaith and although the passing minstrel sired the boy, Rhys raised handsome, kind Dugal as his own beloved son.

Dugal and Niamh, being so close in age, raised together as loving siblings, quickly becoming the best of friends. Soon, the two children had additional playmates. By the end of the very next harvest, Gwen's fertile tree yielded twin fruit, a boy and a girl, both vigorous and healthy. And the following summer, to Rhys's surprise and delight, she bore him yet another son. Two more children followed, for a total of seven and there had never been a happier father and husband in all of Skye.

The year was now 1153. Olaf was dead and Somerled, the Regent of Kinn Tyre, gathered allies in his fastidious plan to claim the throne of Mann. His wife, Olaf's daughter Raghnailt, recently died of pleurisy. Had she been alive, the island kingdom may well have been handed to Somerled uncontested, but as things stood, Olaf's brother-in-law Goraidh declared himself king and Somerled contested this tentative and uncertain line of succession. The powerful warlord had been almost reclusive while his father-in-law alive and in power, but now he recruited followers and would visit to Dunscaith to assure his loyal friend's allegiance.

Somerled, now a widower, was also a most desirable romantic preoccupation for the kingdom's young and eligible maidens. Not only was Somerled dashing and handsome, but the general consensus predicted he would easily prevail against Goraidh in the struggle for the throne. Raghnailt borne him no children and if Somerled won the kingdom, he would need an heir to succeed him. Aware of this necessity, rumor had it he was quite open to considering and pursuing new and exciting amorous alliances.

It was the day of Somerled's visit to Dunscaith and Gwen just returned from a long walk on the beach with her sister. Aillyn recently took up residence at the castle, having no place else to go after the death of their parents.

Gwen happily brought her in, excited to have her friend and confidante so readily available for frequent and valuable sisterly companionship. She and her still youthful and beautiful younger sister remained close over the years, especially since Aillyn never married. Although her suitors were plentiful and requests for her hand frequent, Aillyn invariably refused the countless proposals of marriage.

"You are much too choosy," Gwen often chided, secretly worried her sister would grow old with no husband or children into a sad and lonely spinster, deprived of the happy joys of matrimony and motherhood due to her obsession with a fading memory.

"I simply cannot forget him," Aillyn would reply with a far-off look in her eyes. Gwen would sigh, exasperated yet sympathetic to her sister's fidelity to her romantic ideals. Gwen, after all, sacrificed everything in order to pursue her one true love, so why should her sister, who shared so many of Gwen's viewpoints and attitudes, settle for anything less?

"We are so alike, dear sister!" Gwen would say. "I know you will find him again someday, Aillyn and the day you are reunited with your mysterious and handsome minstrel I will be by your side, crying tears of joy and happiness for your long-awaited reunion."

They were seated now in the reception hall, waiting for Somerled's imminent arrival. Rhys took a small party of soldiers to greet the regent and the battlement lookouts spotted the approaching entourage some time ago. Rhys and the future King of Mann would walk through the door at any moment and the castle was tense with excitement and apprehension.

"I am anxious to meet this thane," said Aillyn, a seductive smile on her face. "I hear he is handsome as well as available, now his wife succumbed to the fever!"

Gwen nodded, making no comment. She was troubled about the regent's visit. Preparations for war already initiated, which meant her husband would soon leave home. Not only would she miss the physical pleasure and loving reassurance of his cock in her pussy, but she feared greatly for his safety.

"Have you ever met him?" Aillyn asked as she looked expectantly towards the door where the Regent of Kinn Tyre and her brother-in-law would soon make their appearance.

Gwen shook her head. "No," she replied. "Although Rhys speaks of him often."

She looked at her sister, smiling as she recognized the all too familiar twinkle of lusty adventure in Aillyn's eyes. "Caution, dear sister," she warned with a laugh. "If you seek the great Somerled's affections, you will not be able to cast him aside like your other fleeting love interests!"

Ailynn shrugged. "I care not for senseless and illogical conventions," she said. "Whether he be a lord or a serf matters little. My darling minstrel stole my heart years ago and he will remain Adonis to my Aphrodite, as long as I live and breathe."

Gwen took her sister's hand, squeezing it with fond tenderness. "One day, another noble contestant for your love might win your heart back from the absent and possessive Adonis," she joked. "Perhaps this Somerled will play Ares to your Aphrodite, my love-struck and star-crossed sister!" she joked.

"If so, I will happily submit to the earnest and pressing sincerity of his hard and convincing masculinity!" she whispered, amused by her own witty and ribald humor.

"You are incorrigible, Sister," Gwen said with good-natured reprimand, as the doors swung open to admit Rhys and his influential and mighty guest.

Gwen and Aillyn looked at each other, the shock and disbelief registered on each of their beautiful faces equally and simultaneously. Gwen glanced again at the approaching party, led by her husband and Somerled; Gwen's face flushed red with a combination of embarrassment and excitement.

Aillyn, wasted no time, pushed back her chair in haste, rushing to greet the small entourage. Rhys, taken by surprise by his sister-in-laws unexpected departure from the usual rules of propriety, stammered the first word or two of an awkward introduction, but it was all too clear Aillyn and the regent were already well-acquainted.

Somerled and Aillyn locked in a passionate embrace, their lips hungry for each other and their bodies entwined as one. Aillyn held the regent's head in her hands as she kissed him, tears of joy running down her quivering cheeks.

Yes, intelligent reader, you have, by now, surmised the obvious truth. Somerled was, in fact, the passing minstrel, disguised all those years ago as a simple bard. His happy reunion with his one true love is yet another story, impatient reader, which, if you insist, I will agree to tell you someday.

Rest assured. The tale is a happy one. Somerled, prevailing in his contest with Goraidh, is ultimately crowned the King of the Isles; Aillyn, his beautiful wife, becomes the first Queen of the Hebrides, Gwen's son Dugal, Somerled's only heir, eventually inherits the kingdom and the two lusty sisters and their willing husbands enjoy many nights of ecstasy together, since, after all, their parents taught them, from a young and tender age, to share and share alike!

So, in the end, true love prevails, as it rightly should. And on this joyful and satisfying note, I rest my pen, my faithful audience and bid you goodnight. Live and love well, loyal reader, until we meet again... soon.

THE END

Lightning Source UK Ltd.
Milton Keynes UK
UKHW040754090820
367940UK00001B/252